The Puzzle at Pineview School

"Before we auction off these beautiful brooches," the headmaster of Pineview School announced to the guests at the charity ball, "Mr. Gideon Ray, a jeweler, will write down their worth and seal the figure in an envelope."

Mr. Ray lifted the velvet cloth off the jewelry.

The crowd gasped in admiration at the pair of antique brooches. "They've been in the Sedgewick family for generations," George whispered to Nancy.

Mr. Ray picked up one of the brooches. He placed a jeweler's magnifying glass in his eye and examined the beautiful gem at the center of the brooch. The air was thick with excitement.

Mr. Ray examined the brooch under the magnifying glass a second time. Then a third. Finally he stepped back. He looked very upset.

"I can't appraise these," he said in a shaken voice. "They aren't real. They're . . . they're worthless fakes!"

Nancy Drew
Mystery Stories

#57 The Triple Hoax
#58 The Flying Saucer Mystery
#59 The Secret in the Old Lace
#60 The Greek Symbol Mystery
#61 The Swami's Ring
#62 The Kachina Doll Mystery
#63 The Twin Dilemma
#64 Captive Witness
#65 Mystery of the Winged Lion
#66 Race Against Time
#67 The Sinister Omen
#68 The Elusive Heiress
#69 Clue in the Ancient Disguise
#70 The Broken Anchor
#71 The Silver Cobweb
#72 The Haunted Carousel
#73 Enemy Match
#74 The Mysterious Image
#75 The Emerald-eyed Cat Mystery
#76 The Eskimo's Secret
#77 The Bluebeard Room
#78 The Phantom of Venice
#79 The Double Horror of Fenley Place
#80 The Case of the Disappearing
      Diamonds
#81 The Mardi Gras Mystery
#82 The Clue in the Camera
#83 The Case of the Vanishing Veil
#84 The Joker's Revenge

#85 The Secret of Shady Glen
#86 The Mystery of Misty Canyon
#87 The Case of the Rising Stars
#88 The Search for Cindy Austin
#89 The Case of the Disappearing
      Deejay
#90 The Puzzle at Pineview School
#91 The Girl Who Couldn't Remember
#92 The Ghost of Craven Cove
#93 The Case of the Safecracker's
      Secret
#94 The Picture-Perfect Mystery
#95 The Silent Suspect
#96 The Case of the Photo Finish
#97 The Mystery at Magnolia Mansion
#98 The Haunting of Horse Island
#99 The Secret at Seven Rocks
#100 A Secret in Time
#101 The Mystery of the Missing
      Millionairess
#102 A Secret in the Dark
#103 The Stranger in the Shadows
#104 The Mystery of the Jade Tiger
#105 The Clue in the Antique Trunk
#106 The Case of the Artful Crime
#107 The Legend of Miner's Creek
#108 The Secret of the Tibetan Treasure
#109 The Mystery of the Masked Rider
#110 The Nutcracker Ballet Mystery
#111 The Secret at Solaire

Available from MINSTREL Books

NANCY DREW®

THE PUZZLE AT PINEVIEW SCHOOL

CAROLYN KEENE

A MINSTREL® BOOK

PUBLISHED BY POCKET BOOKS

New York   London   Toronto   Sydney   Tokyo   Singapore

A MINSTREL PAPERBACK *ORIGINAL*

 A Minstrel Book published by
POCKET BOOKS, a division of Simon & Schuster Inc.
1230 Avenue of the Americas, New York, NY 10020

Copyright © 1989 by Simon & Schuster Inc.
Produced by Mega-Books of New York Inc.

ISBN: 0-671-66315-1

First Minstrel Books printing August 1989

10 9 8 7 6 5 4 3

NANCY DREW, NANCY DREW MYSTERY STORIES,
A MINSTREL BOOK and colophon are registered trademarks
of Simon & Schuster Inc.

Cover art by Aleta Jenks

Printed in the U.S.A.

Contents

1	*The Soccer Ball*	1
2	*Stolen Jewels*	11
3	*Rivalry on the Field*	20
4	*Suspect*	29
5	*The Best Defense Is a Good Offense*	39
6	*Strange Behavior*	50
7	*Trapped!*	60
8	*Where's Kelly?*	67
9	*Hustle and High Fives*	76
10	*A Team in Trouble*	86
11	*Too Few Clues*	98
12	*All Aboard*	107
13	*Hot Pursuit*	114
14	*Carried Away*	122
15	*A Close Call*	129
16	*Cut to the Chase*	137
17	*The Canadian Cup*	146

1

The Soccer Ball

"Nancy, watch out!"

Nancy Drew instinctively put her hand up to protect her face. A red-and-white soccer ball glanced off her arm and fell back onto the soft grass of Pineview School's practice field.

"That was close," said Nancy's friend Bess Marvin. "I told you sports could be dangerous."

"Dangerous?" Nancy laughed and tossed her reddish blond hair over her shoulder. "With lightning-fast reactions, I was born to play soccer."

She picked up the ball and threw it to Bess's cousin George Fayne, who stood waiting in the middle of the field with her all-girl soccer team. George, a tall eighteen-year-old girl in a gray sweat suit, caught the ball easily. Then she blew her whistle to signal the end of practice and jogged toward Nancy and Bess, who stood on the sidelines.

"Sorry, Nancy." George joined them, a little out of breath. "The ball just got away from the girls."

Nancy grinned playfully. "I see, Ms. Assistant Coach. I just thought that was the way the Pineview Giants always ended their practice sessions—by bashing innocent bystanders on the head with the soccer ball."

George laughed. "Hey, you haven't seen anything yet. Wait till we win the Canadian Cup."

"Nancy told me about that," Bess said. "Does the team really have a shot at the championship?"

George shrugged. "It's touch and go right now. If we win the next game, we'll go to Canada for the playoffs. But it will be our first tournament ever and the competition is very tough. We'll need to work up a lot of spirit if we're going to have a chance."

"Well, the girls look great." Nancy patted her friend on the back. "If you need an extra goalie, let me know."

"Yeah, right." George laughed.

"Somehow I don't think she respects us as athletes," Bess remarked.

"I always appreciate your stopping by." George ran a hand through her short, dark brown curls. "Speaking of which, are you ready for the Soccer Ball tonight?"

"Are you kidding? I can't wait," Bess replied, her face pink with excitement. "I bought a new formal gown for the occasion. It's not every day we get to mix with River Heights's high society crowd."

"This is more than just a dance, though, isn't it?" Nancy asked George. "You mentioned some sort of fund-raising activity."

George nodded. "They're going to auction off some jewels that were donated by one of the parents," she said. "The money will go to Pineview School, but part of it's reserved just for the soccer program. That's because the woman who donated the jewels has a daughter on our team. In fact, she's our star goalie."

"The pretty blond girl?" Nancy asked. "I was watching her. She's really good."

Nancy's gaze wandered to the playing field. "Who's that?" she asked George.

George looked where Nancy was pointing. A dark-haired woman in a blue sweat suit trudged slowly toward the gym from the sidelines. Her arms were crossed over her chest, and she was scowling at the ground as she walked.

A frown crossed George's face. "That's my boss," she said. "Katrina Boggs. At the moment, she's the one hitch in our big plan for success."

"Is something wrong with her?" Bess asked. "She looks upset."

"Beats me," said George. "Kate's been like that lately. It's beginning to worry me. I mean, she's a great coach, but when she gets upset, her behavior affects the team." George shrugged. "Maybe she has problems at home."

"Or love problems," Bess suggested.

George and Nancy exchanged smiles. Bess loved romance and tended to see it everywhere she looked.

"Well, if that's what it is," George said, "maybe at the dance tonight we'll meet the man who's causing them. But right now let's go get some ice cream. I, for one, have earned a big reward."

Nancy arrived home late that afternoon. She raced to her room to take out the long gown she was planning to wear. It had gotten a little crushed in the closet and needed to be pressed.

"What's going on?" Hannah Gruen, the Drews' housekeeper, followed Nancy into her room. "Do you have a date with Ned tonight?" Ned was Nancy's longtime boyfriend, and Hannah considered him almost a part of the family.

"Ned's not coming home this weekend." Nancy raced to the laundry room to set up the ironing board. "I'm going to the Soccer Ball at Pineview School with George and Bess. And I'm running late!"

"Oh, the Soccer Ball." Hannah smiled. "Your father called to say he'll be attending that, too. So you'll see each other at the dance."

4

"If I ever get there." Nancy plugged in the iron. "George and Bess are supposed to meet me here at seven o'clock, and I still have to shower and—"

"You'll make it, don't worry," Hannah interrupted, taking the dress from Nancy. "You go get ready. I'll press your gown."

Nancy smiled gratefully at Hannah. Nancy's mother had died when Nancy was a young child, and, ever since, the housekeeper had been as devoted as a parent to her. "Thanks, Hannah. You're a lifesaver."

Hannah laughed. "Save your thanks for more important things," she said. "I remember what it's like to be a young lady going to a dance."

Nancy did look the perfect young lady in her slim floor-length gown as she and her friends arrived at the entrance to Pineview's Lester Auditorium and Banquet Hall. Her hair was twisted into a simple chignon at the nape of her neck, and her blue eyes sparkled with excitement. Bess looked charming, too, in a frilly peach-colored gown, and George's deep green velvet dress set off her dark hair perfectly.

"Ready?" Nancy winked at Bess as they pushed open the heavy oak doors. "Here come the River Heights heartbreakers!"

The banquet hall had been renovated the year before with money donated by the parents of a Pineview student. Inside, it looked elegant and

5

new. The wood paneling gleamed. The marble floor reflected the tiny lights of a dozen chandeliers. A ten-piece orchestra played at one end of the room while couples danced.

The girls stood together at the entrance and watched the women in sparkling, expensive dresses, chatting with men in tuxedos as they nibbled on refreshments. Despite the soccer theme, this dance was clearly an important social affair.

"Here are the three loveliest young ladies I've seen all night." A man in an elegantly tailored dinner jacket approached the girls with a smile.

Bess giggled. "Oh, Mr. Drew, you always flatter us."

"What flattery?" The handsome criminal lawyer held up his hands in protest. "It's the honest truth."

Nancy smiled and slipped her hand into the crook of her father's arm.

"Are you going to bid in the auction, Mr. Drew?" George asked.

"It's a bit too rich for my blood, I'm afraid," the lawyer answered. "They're auctioning a pair of very valuable antique brooches. The school even brought in a highly respected jeweler from Chicago to swear that the jewels are worth a fortune before the bidding begins."

"Sounds exciting," Nancy said.

"Well, just don't get any ideas, Nancy," Mr.

Drew said playfully. Then he excused himself and rejoined his friends.

"Oh, look, there's Coach Boggs," George said to the girls. "Come on, I'll introduce you."

George led them over to the refreshment table where the pretty, dark-haired coach was getting a glass of punch. Katrina Boggs was in her early thirties. She had an athletic build, sharp facial features, and strikingly high cheekbones—and she wore the same worried expression that Nancy had noticed on the soccer field that afternoon.

"Coach Boggs," George said, "I'd like you to meet my cousin Bess Marvin. And this is my good friend, Nancy Drew."

As Coach Boggs turned toward the girls, the stress lines around her close-set brown eyes seemed to soften.

"Call me Kate, please," she said with a nervous smile.

"According to George, you're quite a coach, Kate," Nancy said, trying to put the woman at ease. "She says you're the main reason the team has done so well during the past two years. I hope you make it all the way to Canada."

"Thanks, Nancy," Kate said. "And according to George, you're quite a detective. She's told me all about you, too."

"I guess we can't keep any secrets with George around," said Nancy with a laugh.

"What has she said about me?" Bess asked. She gave George a curious look.

"She says you're a good friend, even though you told her she's crazy to coach a high school soccer team," Kate said.

Bess blushed, and they all laughed.

Just then a cart was wheeled out onto the center of the marble floor directly beneath a large chandelier. A thin, tight-lipped man stepped up to the cart. He signaled the orchestra to stop playing. Couples broke off dancing, and a hush fell over the crowd.

"Is that the headmaster?" Nancy whispered to George, gesturing toward the man beside the cart.

George nodded. "Russell Garrison."

"He looks as if he hasn't smiled in a month," Bess commented in a low voice.

"Sssh," George hissed. "Someone will hear you." She looked around. "So far, I think he likes me."

When the crowd had settled down, Russell Garrison took a microphone from the cart and cleared his throat. He was very well dressed, and seemed at ease among the wealthy people who surrounded him. "You all know why we're here," he told the audience. "But many of you may not know who gave us the lovely jewelry we're about to auction. I'd like to introduce the donor, Mrs. Ellen Sedgewick."

"Janine's mother," George murmured as a prim, middle-aged woman in a simple white gown smiled and waved. Mrs. Sedgewick's smile was lovely, and her eyes shone with excitement. The onlookers applauded.

"The money from Mrs. Sedgewick's gift will go to two very worthy causes," Mr. Garrison continued. "It should nearly double Pineview's scholarship fund, and it will also benefit our soon-to-be-champion soccer team, the Pineview Giants. Let's hear it for the Canadian Cup!" The crowd applauded and cheered.

"Now." Mr. Garrison cleared his throat dramatically. "Let me introduce Mr. Gideon Ray, a jeweler with the Chicago firm of Holder and Canfield. He examined the jewelry just this morning and will now write down the worth of the brooches and seal the figure in this envelope. After the auction we'll hand the envelope over to the highest bidder. Mr. Ray?"

Mr. Garrison held out a white envelope for the stocky, balding man at his side. Mr. Ray took it and stepped briskly to the cart. He lifted the velvet cloth off the jewelry.

The crowd gasped in admiration as they gazed at the pair of antique brooches. Their colored gemstones sparkled in the bright light. Their intricate settings were made of gold. "Janine says they've been in her family for generations," George whispered to her friends.

When everyone had gotten a good look, Mr. Ray picked up one of the brooches. He placed a jeweler's magnifying glass in his eye and began examining the beautiful gem at the center of the brooch.

The air was thick with excitement. Nancy watched as the man held the brooch up higher to get the full benefit of the strong lights.

Suddenly Mr. Ray's face registered surprise. He turned the brooch over, then lowered it and flipped it over a second time, then a third. Finally he stepped back and removed the glass from his eye. He looked very upset.

Instinctively, Nancy edged closer to the cart to hear what the jeweler had to say.

Mr. Garrison moved closer, too. "They certainly are beautiful, aren't they?" he said. "Now, Mr. Ray, if you'll write down what they're worth and seal the envelope, we'll proceed with the auction."

Mr. Ray stood for a moment without moving.

"I—I can't," the stocky man stammered.

"Can't?" repeated the bewildered Mr. Garrison. "What do you mean, you can't?"

"I can't appraise these. They aren't real. They're . . . they're worthless fakes!"

2

Stolen Jewels

The audience gasped as Gideon Ray put down his magnifying glass. Then everyone fell silent. Ellen Sedgewick ran to the cart and snatched up the glittering brooches.

"That's impossible!" she said in a panicky voice. "These are *my* brooches. They've been in my family for more than seventy years!"

"Mr. Ray, there must be some mistake," Russell Garrison said. "You officially examined these pieces this morning. Now, just hours later, you're telling us they're fakes. Please examine them again."

"Mr. Garrison," Mr. Ray said, "I've been looking at jewelry for a long time. These are not the brooches I saw earlier today. Those were genu-

11

ine. These are fakes. They're good copies, but they're made of paste."

By this time Nancy had worked her way to the front of the crowd. She was joined by her father and Bess. George stayed behind with a shy-looking girl with long blond hair. The girl looked very upset. Nancy recognized her from soccer practice. She was Mrs. Sedgewick's daughter, Janine.

Mrs. Sedgewick examined the jewels herself through the magnifying glass while Gideon Ray pointed something out to her. The woman turned pale. Her hand trembled as she held the brooch and nodded. Finally, she turned to Russell Garrison.

"Russell, I think we'd better call the police. Mr. Ray is right. These brooches are copies."

Garrison nodded and then picked up the microphone. "My apologies, ladies and gentlemen," he said, obviously embarrassed. "We have a problem that must be cleared up before the auction. Please go back to your dancing, and enjoy yourselves."

But the mood of the party had been spoiled. Many people left. Others stood talking in small groups about what had taken place.

Nancy saw her father approach Ellen Sedgewick, whom he apparently knew quite well. Nancy and Bess joined George, Coach Boggs, and Janine.

"Don't worry, Janine," George was saying.

12

"Nancy will help your mother solve this mystery."

"Not so fast," Nancy protested. She smiled uncomfortably at the pretty but worried-looking girl. "This looks like a very clever jewel theft, but the police should be able to solve it."

"I'm not worried about that," Janine objected. "I'm worried about my mother."

Nancy's eyebrows went up in surprise. "Why?" she asked. "Is she in trouble?"

"What if the police think she was involved in the theft of the real jewels?" Janine asked worriedly.

"Why would they suspect your mother of stealing her own jewels?" Bess sounded bewildered. "It doesn't make sense."

"It's been done before," Nancy said. "Sometimes dishonest people pretend their precious jewels have been stolen so they can collect the insurance money. That way they have both the jewels and the money."

She turned to Janine. "But there's no reason to think the police would suspect your mother of insurance fraud. Is there?"

Janine shook her head. She wiped tears from her eyes and pushed her hair away from her face.

Nancy smiled at the girl. "Tell you what. I've worked with the police before, and they know me. If I find out anything, I'll let you know. How's that?"

"Thank you, Nancy. I really appreciate it."

Janine sniffed and smiled at Nancy. Then she held out her hand. Nancy shook it.

"Janine, I'll take you back to your room in the dorm to freshen up a little," Kate said. "Those tears have smeared your makeup. You don't want your mother to see you like this."

Janine sniffed again. "Okay, Coach. But let's hurry so I can come back and be with her."

Kate put her arm around Janine and left the hall with her.

"Coach Boggs is really being nice," Bess said to George.

"She is nice, but she's also protecting the team," George answered. "Janine has meant a lot to us this year. Kate knows she won't play her best if she's upset."

"That makes sense," Nancy said. "But I wonder why Janine is so worried about her mother. Why should anyone suspect Mrs. Sedge-wick?"

"Janine is probably just in shock because of what happened," Bess suggested.

"Maybe," Nancy said. "But it's a strange conclusion for her to jump to." She shook her head. "I hope for Janine's sake the police lock this case up quickly."

"Oh, no! Did you say 'lock'?" George sounded so distressed that her two friends turned to look at her. "I think I forgot to lock the equipment room this afternoon."

"How could you forget?" Bess asked.

George frowned. "I was in such a hurry that I think I forgot."

"You'd better go check," said Nancy.

George ran off without another word. As she left the banquet hall, two police officers and a detective entered. Russell Garrison led them across the room to Gideon Ray and Mrs. Sedgewick.

Nancy saw her father look at her. Then Carson Drew walked over to join the two girls.

"This could be a messy one," he said. "Those jewels were worth a lot of money."

"How much?" Nancy asked.

"Apparently, Mr. Ray appraised them this morning at more than one hundred thousand dollars. It looks as if he wasn't the only one who knew what they were worth. This seems to have been a very well planned robbery. And if Mr. Garrison hadn't invited the jeweler to be here tonight to make the auction more dramatic, the switch might never have been discovered."

"Switch?" asked Bess. She looked confused.

"Someone took the real jewels and substituted the fakes," Mr. Drew explained.

"That means that whoever did it knew exactly what the real brooches looked like and hired an expert to make the fake jewelry," Nancy added.

"Exactly," said her father.

"How do you know Mrs. Sedgewick, Dad?"

"I've met her a few times at charity functions. I've known her family for a long time."

"Her daughter is worried that the police might suspect Mrs. Sedgewick of stealing the jewels herself to get the insurance money," Bess said. "Isn't that ridiculous? Why would such a rich woman steal her own jewels? Especially after she had donated them to the school?"

"It may not be as ridiculous as it sounds," said Mr. Drew in a low voice. "I know I can trust you girls to keep this quiet. Mrs. Sedgewick decided to donate the jewels to Pineview several months ago. Since then, she's lost quite a large part of her fortune."

"So she needs money," Nancy said.

"Exactly. And she stands to collect quite a large insurance payment on those brooches if they're not found."

Nancy nodded. "I see what you're saying, Dad. The police might smell a motive. That's why Janine was upset."

The girls turned to watch the police question Mr. Ray and Mrs. Sedgewick. Nancy had seen Detective Ryan work before. She knew he was very thorough. As she and Bess watched, one of the police officers put the fake brooches in small plastic bags. Nancy knew they would be examined for fingerprints later.

Detective Ryan spotted Carson Drew and the two girls. He walked over. The detective wore a stern expression. He knew Nancy's reputation. And Nancy knew he didn't like other people interfering in police matters.

"Carson," he said to Mr. Drew, "are you representing someone in this little caper?"

Carson Drew smiled. "Believe it or not, Jim, I came here tonight strictly for fun."

"I'm sure," Ryan said. He glanced at Nancy. "And you, Ms. Drew? Are you by any chance looking for a new and challenging case?"

"Not this time."

"Our friend coaches the soccer team here," Bess blurted out.

Ryan nodded. "Well, I think we'll wrap this one up pretty fast. The jewels can't be too far away yet, and we're pretty sure who's responsible for the switch." He started off. "See you around," he said.

"What did he mean by that?" Bess asked when he was gone.

"He means there aren't many suspects," said Nancy. "Not many people knew about the auction, for one thing. Even fewer knew what the brooches looked like, how they'd be handled, or when they'd be brought to the school. So the thief is most likely someone who helped to plan the fund-raising auction."

"Someone like Mrs. Sedgewick," Bess said quietly.

"Someone close to the situation," Nancy said. She frowned, thinking hard.

"Okay, girls," said Mr. Drew. "Let's not get carried away. I think it's time for me to call it a night."

"I guess we'll leave as soon as George gets back," Nancy said.

Carson Drew nodded and gave his daughter a peck on the cheek. "I'll see you at home," he said.

Carson Drew had just left when Bess said, "Hasn't George been gone for an awfully long time?"

Nancy nodded. "Let's go find her."

The girls left the banquet hall and walked across the campus to the gym. They pushed open the front door and went inside.

"George?" Nancy called. The gym was very dark inside, lit only by the red exit signs over the doors.

"I've never seen the equipment room," Nancy said. She peered around in the darkness. "Maybe it's down here." She pointed to a narrow stairway leading into the basement.

"That's the only place it could be," Bess agreed. "Let's go."

It was even darker on the steep metal stairway than on the main floor of the gym. A shiver went up Nancy's spine as she descended the stairs. She smiled at her reaction to the spooky place. "Thank goodness," she said to Bess, who followed behind her. "There's a light on down here."

A single bare light bulb hung from the ceiling of a narrow corridor that ran beneath the gym floor. Heavy doors, painted dull gray, were evenly spaced along its length.

Nancy strode down the corridor quickly. Bess stayed close behind her.

When they reached the third door on the left, they saw that it was wide open.

"I guess George was right." Bess sounded relieved. "She did forget to lock the room. I wonder where she is."

"I don't know." Nancy entered the dark room. "There must be a light some—"

Nancy stopped short. She had stumbled on something near the entrance. Not something—someone. She found the light switch and turned it on.

Behind her, Bess gasped. "It's George—and she's unconscious!"

3

Rivalry on the Field

Nancy knelt and quickly felt for George's pulse.
As Bess looked on anxiously, George came to.

"Wha—what happened?" she stammered.
She sat up straight and rubbed the back of her
head.

"That's what we want to know," Nancy said.

"We came down here looking for you," said
Bess. "How'd you wind up on the floor? Did
someone hit you?"

"I'm not sure," George answered. She looked
and sounded groggy.

"Maybe she tripped," Bess said to Nancy.
"Look, that bucket is tipped over."

A custodian's mop pail lay on its side by the
door. The mop handle had fallen into the hall.

"Looks as if you fell over the mop," said Nancy. "Is that what happened, George?"

"Nan, I can't remember. Maybe I tripped. I think I heard a noise. It was just after I came down here. I saw that the door was locked and I—"

"But it's not locked," Bess said. "Not now."

George looked around, confused. "But it was locked." She rubbed her head. "At least, I think it was."

Just then a loud voice shouted, "Hey, who's in there?"

It was a woman's voice, coming from the corridor.

"It's me, Coach," George called.

Kate Boggs appeared in the doorway. She saw George on the floor and rushed to her side. "What happened to you?" she demanded.

After George had told the coach all she remembered, Nancy asked, "Should anyone besides you and George be down here at this time of night?"

"Definitely not," Kate said. "Once in a while George and I have to come down for something. But the equipment room is always locked—even during the day, except before and after practice."

"Who has a key?" Nancy asked.

"I do, of course. And George, and the custodian, Mr. Quinn. The headmaster has a master key, but I doubt that Russell Garrison would ever come down here."

As they talked, George got to her feet.

"You sure you're all right?" Bess asked.

"Yeah, I'm fine," George said. She rubbed the back of her head gently. "Just shaken up a little. I'll be okay."

"Good." Nancy turned to Kate. "Can you tell if anything's missing?"

Kate glanced around the room. "Everything seems to be in place," she said. "I can't be completely sure."

"Maybe this wasn't just an accident," Bess said.

"Exactly what I was thinking," Nancy said. "Kate, do you mind my asking what you're doing down here so late at night?"

"Nancy!" George gasped.

Kate gave Nancy a surprised smile. "It's all right, George, that's a fair question," she said. "Our game uniforms were supposed to be returned from the laundry today. I just wanted to make sure they got back in time." She looked around. "Yes, they're here." She nodded past Nancy at the stack of uniforms on a nearby table.

Nancy smiled, as if to say she hoped there were no hard feelings. "Mind if I stop by to watch the practice tomorrow?" she asked. "I want to see more of this championship team."

"We'd love to have you." Coach Boggs sounded as though she were answering a challenge.

"I think we'd better get George home," Bess said. "She still looks shaky to me."

"Good idea," said Nancy.

The Sunday papers all ran front-page stories on the clever jewel theft. The inside pages featured interviews with Russell Garrison and Gideon Ray.

"I don't like the way this article is worded," Nancy said to her father as they sat reading the paper at the kitchen table. "First it says that Mrs. Sedgewick is thought to have severe money problems. Then it says the jewels were heavily insured. It says next that she refuses to comment on the theft. That suggests that Mrs. Sedgewick had a good reason to steal her own jewels."

"Just because she could have used the insurance money doesn't mean she stole the jewels," Mr. Drew replied. He shook his head sadly. "I don't know, though. I'd be surprised if she wasn't Detective Ryan's prime suspect right now." He gave his daughter a stern look. "That still doesn't mean *you* have to get involved."

Nancy thought about the case later that day as she drove to soccer practice. Her father had been right when he suspected her of getting caught up in the mystery. It was true—she really wanted to find out who had stolen the jewels from under so many people's noses.

"Detective Ryan doesn't want you interfering," she reminded herself as she parked her blue

23

sports car in front of the school. But Ryan couldn't keep her from thinking about the case. She smiled as she stepped onto the pavement.

It was a beautiful fall day. There was only a hint of chill in the air. The narrow tree-lined paths that connected the school buildings gave the campus a picture-postcard look. Pineview was more than one hundred years old and had a nationwide reputation for excellence. Some of its students even came from other countries.

When Nancy walked out to the soccer field, the girls were already practicing. This time Coach Boggs was in charge. She had the team running up and down the field, three at a time, while kicking the ball back and forth.

Nancy was again impressed by how well most of the girls handled the soccer ball. George had said Kate Boggs was a great coach. Nancy could see that was true.

Nancy spotted Janine standing by the goal area on the far end of the field. The girl's blond hair shone in the afternoon light. She was talking to a taller girl with dark hair.

Nancy shaded her eyes with her hand and peered across the field at them. It looked as if the two girls were arguing. Janine seemed very upset. The other girl made some wild gestures, as though she was shouting at Janine.

The two girls were interrupted by the sound of Coach Boggs's whistle. Janine instantly came to

24

attention in front of her goal. The other girl trotted to the goal at the opposite end of the field. It looked as if a practice game was about to begin.

George passed by on her way to the far end of the field. She stopped to say hello to Nancy.

"Who's that girl?" Nancy asked. "The other goalie?"

"Kelly Lewis," George answered. "She's good, but not as good as Janine. She's our second-string goalie. That means she doesn't get to play unless Janine is out of the game."

Nancy watched carefully as the practice game began. The players worked the red-and-white ball toward one goal or the other, then tried to kick it into the net. Janine moved back and forth in front of one goal. Dark-haired Kelly protected the other one. Both girls tried hard to keep the ball away from their goal.

Nancy remembered how quick Janine had been at tending goal on Saturday. But Nancy saw no fancy footwork today. Janine looked bored and distracted. Too many easy shots got past her. Meanwhile, Kelly Lewis made several leaping and diving saves. She even won a round of cheers from her teammates.

Toward the end of the game, Nancy saw Coach Boggs approach Janine and ask her something. Janine shook her head. The coach left, and less than a minute later Janine missed another easy shot.

"What's wrong with Janine?" Nancy asked when George and Kate joined her after the game. The girls on the soccer team were running two laps around the field to stretch their muscles. "She didn't play half as well today as she did yesterday."

"I don't know what's wrong with her," Kate said. She frowned into the distance. "She sure isn't herself today. That bothers me."

"What bothers me," George grumbled, "is that if Janine doesn't play well, our chances of winning the Canadian Cup are practically zero."

"She's that important to the team?" asked Nancy.

"Oh, yes." Kate nodded. "Janine is a top-notch goalie. She plays like a professional. That gives any team a big advantage."

"What about Kelly Lewis?" Nancy asked.

"Kelly would be tops on a lot of teams," Kate said with a sigh, "but she's never been as good as Janine."

"Does that bother her?"

"Kelly can be a hothead," Kate admitted. "She's very competitive and wishes she could be our first-string goalie. Of course, any athlete worth her salt thinks she should play every game."

Just as the girls were finishing their laps, Nancy and the others heard Janine yell, "Leave me alone, Kelly! You have no right to say that!"

"Why? Does the truth hurt?" Kelly shouted back. "Everyone at school is talking about it. Even the newspaper said your mother needs money."

By the time Kate, George, and Nancy reached the two girls, they had started shoving each other. Kelly had a faint smile on her face, as though she enjoyed the confrontation. But Janine looked close to tears.

"I won't have this behavior on my team," Coach Boggs said as she pulled the girls apart. "Especially now."

"Then tell her to keep her opinions to herself!" Janine cried.

"Hey, it isn't my mother who needs money so bad she has to steal from the school."

"Kelly, stop that!" Coach Boggs snapped. "No one knows who took those jewels Saturday night."

"Kelly will do anything to upset me, just so she can take my place in a game," Janine said to the coach.

"Both of you girls had better remember that this is a team," Coach Boggs said sternly. "I'll be happy to get rid of anyone who works against the team's spirit. Understand?"

Janine and Kelly nodded sheepishly. Then Kelly headed for the showers. Along the way she stopped to talk with a couple of her teammates.

"She's never going to leave me alone, Coach, I

just know it," Janine said in a low voice. "She started in on my mother the minute we got to practice today."

Coach Boggs sighed. "I'll talk to her again." She turned to Nancy and George. "See you two later."

Coach Boggs trotted briskly after Kelly. Nancy approached Janine. "Are you all right?" she asked.

The girl sniffed. "All I can think about is the jewel theft. I *knew* if people found out we need money right now they'd start to think my mother might—" Janine blinked back her tears and looked at Nancy. "Do you think my mother stole those brooches?" she asked. "I mean, it looks so bad. . . ."

Nancy knew what Janine meant. The case was so mystifying that Janine was wondering about her own mother.

"I just have to know what really happened," Janine said. "Won't you find out who did it, Nancy? Even if you can't catch the thief, maybe you could at least prove my mother is innocent. Please, Nancy."

What Janine didn't know was that, in her own mind at least, Nancy had taken up the case the day before. Now was her chance to make it official.

"All right." Nancy smiled sympathetically and patted Janine's shoulder. "You win, Janine. I'll take the case."

4

Suspect

It was late afternoon when George and Nancy left Pineview School. They were going to stop and pick up Bess before heading to Nancy's house. Nancy was anxious to talk to her father.

"You don't really think there's a chance Mrs. Sedgewick is a thief, do you?" George asked.

"I don't know who stole the brooches," said Nancy. "My hunch is that Mrs. Sedgewick is innocent, but I've got to learn more about the case before I can be sure. Anyway, if she is involved, I don't think Janine knows anything about it."

"I'd hate to think Mrs. Sedgewick is dishonest," George said. "Janine really looks up to her mother."

"George, how big a deal is this Canadian Cup Tournament?" Nancy asked.

"Very big," George said. "It's open to a large number of private schools in the United States and Canada. Most of them are old and wealthy, like Pineview. Kate mentioned once that winning the cup would do more than just bring honor to the school. She says the school's alumnae are very competitive about the tournament. A victory would mean more alumnae donations to the school."

"Hmm. Interesting," Nancy said. "I suppose the alumnae of the other schools feel the same way. What if someone wanted to ensure that a certain school won the Canadian Cup? What would be the best way to make sure Pineview lost?"

"Janine's our strongest player," George said right away. "Without her we probably couldn't win."

George's eyes widened. "Nan, you don't think someone would try to frame Mrs. Sedgewick just to upset Janine," she said.

"It's farfetched, I admit," said Nancy. "But we've got to look at all the angles. I'll know more after I've talked to Dad and Mrs. Sedgewick and Mr. Garrison."

"But if someone is trying to ruin the team's chances and this trick doesn't work," George said, "then Janine might be in some kind of danger."

"I know," said Nancy. "That's one reason we need to work fast."

Carson Drew was at home when the three girls arrived. The radio was playing softly.

"Anything new on the jewel theft, Dad?" Nancy asked as she, George, and Bess entered the living room.

"Not yet. The police are questioning everyone connected with the jewels and the auction."

"How much do you know about the Sedgewicks' money problems?"

Nancy's businesslike tone of voice was all too familiar to her father. "Nancy, are you—"

"Janine Sedgewick begged me to help. She's afraid someone will accuse her mother of stealing the jewels to get the insurance money."

Carson Drew leaned forward and turned off the radio. He looked tired. "Nancy, you know Detective Ryan doesn't want you on this case. This is a big-time robbery, and—"

"I know that, Dad. That's why it's important that I work on the case. We think someone might have taken the jewels to upset Janine Sedgewick enough to ruin Pineview's chances of winning the Canadian Cup."

"Hmmm." Mr. Drew looked surprised. "I hadn't thought of that."

"You see? They need me," Nancy insisted. She smiled so confidently that Mr. Drew had to grin in spite of his doubts.

"Well, then, I suppose all I can do is try to help."

Nancy, George, and Bess sat down in the living room to listen to Carson Drew's story. "Janine's father was a very successful businessman. He died about three years ago," he began. "At the time it looked as though he had made his family's future secure. But most of the money he left them was in stocks, instead of cash in the bank. About six months ago, a big chunk of the stocks plunged in value. They became almost worthless overnight. Ellen Sedgewick can't sell them, so she suddenly finds herself almost broke."

"Can't she just hold on to the stocks until they're worth something again?" Bess asked.

"Sure," Mr. Drew answered. "But in the meantime, she has very little money to pay her bills with. That's why she was talking to me at the ball. She wanted me to give her the name of a good accountant to help her find a way out of this mess."

Nancy nodded thoughtfully. "Did you get the feeling she was trying to hide anything?"

"Not at all. I think she wants to straighten everything out. With good planning I hope she'll be able to get back on her feet."

"Did she mention the brooches when she talked to you?"

Carson Drew took a deep breath. "Yes. She told me that the brooches had been sitting in a vault for years. And now, when she would have liked to sell them, she had already promised them to the school."

"So the cash from the insurance would be very helpful."

"No doubt about it. But I'm sure the insurance company will check out her story thoroughly before they pay such a big claim."

"Unfortunately," Nancy said, "she does have a very strong motive for theft."

"I'm sure the police are investigating carefully," Mr. Drew said. "But they can't arrest her without evidence."

"Then we've got to hurry," Nancy said. "The team plays its last game Tuesday. If they win, they'll soon be on their way to Canada."

"We're playing the Forsythe School next," George said. "It will be an easy game. We can win it without Janine if we have to. Getting into the tournament is practically a sure thing."

Nancy nodded thoughtfully. "This case may be tougher than I thought," she said. "I guess it's time for some good old-fashioned legwork."

Bright and early the next morning Nancy entered the Pineview School's main office and asked to see Russell Garrison. She gave his secretary her name and said she wanted to speak to him about the jewel theft. After a long wait, she was told to go in.

There was another man with Russell Garrison in his large, elegant office. Nancy got the feeling that the two men had been arguing right before she entered. Now they both stood stiffly in front of Mr. Garrison's desk, looking at her.

Russell Garrison was neatly dressed in a blue suit and dark tie. His graying hair was close-cropped.

The other man was older and less well dressed. He looked nervous and out of place in the elegant room.

"Ms. Drew, come in," Mr. Garrison said. "I understand you're Carson Drew's daughter. He and I have met several times. Always a pleasure."

Garrison shook Nancy's hand firmly. Then he turned to the older man.

"This is Jonathan Morse. He's been the art teacher here since . . . well, let's just say for a very long time. He's one of Pineview's most popular teachers."

"Pleased to meet you, Mr. Morse," Nancy said.

"You're not a Pineview girl," Mr. Morse said. "I remember all my girls."

"No. I went to River Heights High."

"A shame," the old man said. "We've got an excellent school here. Maybe you'll send your daughter to us someday."

Nancy smiled. The old man was charming. "Maybe," she said. "If I have a daughter someday."

"Well, I must get to my first class," Mr. Morse said. "Haven't missed one in nearly fifty years."

After Jonathan Morse left, Nancy noticed that
Garrison relaxed a bit and looked much more at
ease. He motioned to Nancy to have a seat. He
then walked around his large oak desk and sat
down.

"Is that true?" Nancy asked. "He hasn't
missed a class in all that time?"

"Almost," the headmaster said. "He's an institution, all right. Now, my secretary said you
wanted to talk about the unfortunate theft we
had the other night. How may I help you?"

"Janine Sedgewick has asked me to look into
the jewel theft. She feels that people might
suspect her mother. She's sure Mrs. Sedgewick
had nothing to do with it."

"*You're* looking into it? Ms. Drew, isn't this a
matter for the police?"

"I'm a detective, Mr. Garrison. Although I'm
not a professional, I've solved some tough cases."

Garrison nodded his head slowly.

"Yes, yes, now it all comes back," he said.
"Pineview business takes up most of my time, but
I do remember reading about you in the past. A
detective. Well, as I said, how may I help you?"

"I need to know exactly when the jewels were
brought to the school." Nancy pulled a notebook
and pen from her purse. "And how they were
handled right up to the moment when Mr. Ray
made his discovery."

Garrison's eyebrows shot up at Nancy's

superefficient attitude, but he began talking anyway. "Ellen brought the brooches in to show us several months ago, when she first decided to donate them to the school," he said. "She took them home with her that day and didn't bring them back until the morning of the Soccer Ball."

He watched Nancy write this down in her notebook. Then he continued. "Mr. Ray made his official appraisal at about eleven o'clock on the morning of the auction. At two o'clock, a group of reporters arrived to ask questions and take photographs. Mrs. Sedgewick was here, and Mr. Ray, plus several other teachers and Coach Boggs."

"Coach Boggs?"

"Certainly. The soccer team would have been given a large sum of money from the auction. We're all proud of the team's progress this year."

"What happened after the photo session?"

"The jewels were placed in a safe in the admissions office. Mr. Ray and I took them out just before we brought them to the ball. And, as they say, you know the rest."

"So the switch had to have been made between Mr. Ray's appraisal at eleven in the morning and his next look at them at the ball itself."

"It would seem so, unless . . ."

"Unless what, Mr. Garrison?"

The gray-haired man smiled. "Nothing. Mr. Ray has an excellent reputation. I'm sure his first appraisal was reliable."

Nancy frowned and leaned back in her chair.

"You don't think Mrs. Sedgewick had anything to do with this, do you, Mr. Garrison?"

"Right now, Ms. Drew, I'm only concerned with the embarrassment, the scandal, this whole affair is causing Pineview. This school is my life. I'll do anything to keep it from being hurt."

"All right. Can you think of anyone besides Mrs. Sedgewick who might have a reason to take these jewels?"

Russell Garrison stood up and walked slowly to the window behind his desk. He gazed out over the Pineview campus. His back was to Nancy. He seemed to be trying to decide whether or not to tell her something.

"Ms. Drew," he said finally. "This is very difficult for me to say. I trust that as a detective you will keep confidential whatever I tell you."

"Of course."

He cleared his throat nervously. "I've been having a rather serious problem with one of my teachers. This person borrowed money against her salary twice this year. Just recently this same teacher told me that she was leaving her job at the end of this year. Needless to say, I'm concerned about the money she owes the school. I understand she has other large debts as well. It may be nothing, but . . ."

"Who is the teacher, Mr. Garrison?"

"It's not at all correct for me to tell you her name."

"But it sounds as if you think she might have had a reason to steal the jewels. Mr. Garrison, you owe it to Mrs. Sedgewick to tell me."

Garrison turned to face Nancy. Finally he said, "I'm afraid it's Kate Boggs, the soccer coach, Ms. Drew."

5

The Best Defense Is a Good Offense

Nancy decided to stay at the school until soccer practice began. George had said that the girls would start early today, since the Forsythe game was tomorrow.

She walked the grounds for a while, enjoying the peacefulness of the lovely campus. She wondered what it would have been like to go to school there.

Pineview was more than a rich-girls' school. Most of the students were from wealthy families, but the academic standards were high as well. Pineview graduates had gone on to do well in many different fields. Nancy could understand why Russell Garrison was upset about the scandal caused by the jewel theft.

Feeling refreshed from her stroll, Nancy went to the library. A few girls were studying there. In an empty lounge Nancy noticed Kelly Lewis thumbing through a thick book. She went over to her.

"Hi, Kelly." Nancy sat down facing the younger girl and smiled at her. "Hitting the books early, I see."

Kelly looked up blankly.

"I'm Nancy Drew. A friend of George's . . . uh, Coach Fayne."

Kelly nodded. "Right. I saw you at practice with her."

"Looks as if you girls are headed for Canada. You must be pretty excited about it."

Kelly didn't answer for a second. She looked as though she wasn't sure how friendly she wanted to be. "Looks that way," she said in a dull voice.

Nancy eyed the scowling girl carefully. "If I were on the team, I'd be more excited than you are."

"Watching the game from the bench is nothing to be excited about."

"I can understand that. But then, you never know when you'll be needed. Isn't that part of being on a team?"

Kelly frowned. "I'm ready," she said. "I practice hard. But Coach Boggs seems to prefer the Golden Girl. Ask Coach Fayne. She'll tell you how it is." Kelly's anger toward Janine seemed about to explode.

"I have asked her," Nancy said. "She can't understand why you and Janine don't get along."

"What are you? Some kind of spy for Coach Fayne or Coach Boggs? Everybody knows how Janine and I feel about each other. And I don't like the way she and her mother ripped off the school, either."

"You really think they did that?"

"We all know her mother is broke. Who else would do something like that?"

"That's what I'm trying to find out," Nancy said.

The dark-haired girl stared at Nancy. "You?"

"That's right. I'm a detective." Nancy waited to see Kelly's reaction.

"Is this a joke?"

"Not at all. Janine asked me to find out what really happened."

"Oh, I get it." Kelly closed her book and stood up. "You're just like everyone else. Looking out for poor little Janine. Well, don't expect any help from me."

"I'm not looking for help, Kelly," Nancy said in a calm voice. "I'm looking for the truth."

Kelly snorted and stalked away. Nancy watched her go, thinking about what the girl had said. Then she got up to leave, too.

On her way out of the library, Nancy bumped smack into the art teacher, Jonathan Morse.

"I beg your pardon," the old man said. "I wasn't looking where I was going again. I do that, you know."

Jonathan Morse looked even more absent-minded than he had in Garrison's office.

"It's all right, Mr. Morse." Nancy smiled. "It was just a little bump."

Morse looked relieved. For the first time he realized whom he was talking to. "You're the young lady I met in Mr. Garrison's office, aren't you? The one who should have gone to Pineview!"

Nancy laughed. "If only we could do some things over again."

The old man nodded. A sad, faraway look had come into his eyes. Nancy wondered what he was thinking.

"Even at my age, young lady, there are some things you regret," he said. "Maybe we're never as smart as we think."

Nancy smiled again. "Mr. Morse, you should be very proud of what you've done with your life. Look at all the students you've helped over the years. From what I understand, Pineview really depends on you."

The art teacher's face lit up with pleasure. Then he looked sad again. "I hope so. I depend on it, too, I'm afraid."

Nancy thought she saw a tear in the old man's eye. He certainly loved teaching.

"Well," the teacher said, "I must go. I need some materials for my afternoon lecture."

"I hope we can talk again sometime, Mr. Morse," Nancy said.

"Yes, let's do that. And remember, your daughter *must* be a Pineview girl."

Nancy laughed and shook the old man's hand. He had a strong and sure grip. She liked him, and she could understand why everyone else did, too.

Next, Nancy went to the admissions office to pick up some brochures on the school. She learned that Russell Garrison was in his fifteenth year as headmaster. Jonathan Morse was beginning his forty-sixth year at the old school.

As she read the brochures, Nancy walked slowly to the dining hall. The team would be eating a light meal before practice. George was already there, so Nancy grabbed a yogurt and sat down with her. In a few minutes they were joined by Kate Boggs.

"I didn't think we'd see you again so soon, Nancy," Kate said. "Don't tell me our team has another loyal fan."

"That's part of it," Nancy said. "But I'm also looking into the jewel robbery."

"I keep forgetting your reputation as a detective. I'm sorry."

"You mean I haven't bragged about her enough?" George teased.

"Now that you mention it," Kate teased back.

43

Then she looked up from her food at Nancy with her sharp, birdlike eyes. "Who asked you to investigate the robbery?"

"Janine," Nancy said, putting down her spoon. "She's afraid people will think her mother had something to do with it."

Kate nodded. "I was worried about that. Janine's been so upset over this robbery that it's affected her playing. With the tournament coming up, the last thing we need is for our star goalie to have her mind someplace else."

"So much the better, then, if I can reassure her," Nancy said. "Tell me something, though. If you didn't have Janine, couldn't Kelly Lewis do the job?"

"Maybe. Maybe not. She doesn't have the game experience, because she's always played behind Janine. I think that's why she resents Janine so much."

Nancy glanced at George. She wanted to tell her friend how angry Kelly had been in the library. Surely Kelly wouldn't have stolen the jewelry just to get a chance to help win the Canadian Cup?

The three of them ate quietly for a few minutes, each lost in her own thoughts. Finally, George stood up.

"Time to get the equipment ready for practice," she said. "That's one of the exciting jobs assistant coaches have."

"Yes, and you're a genius at it," Kate teased.

44

"Just think," Nancy added. "Next they'll start letting you iron the team's uniforms."

"That'll be the day."

Kate and Nancy laughed. George shook her head and walked off. Nancy took a few more spoonfuls of yogurt before looking back at Kate.

"I understand you're quitting," she said.

The older woman looked very surprised. "You really are a detective," she said at last. "No one's supposed to know that. And I certainly wouldn't want the team to know. Especially just before the playoffs."

"I'm not going to tell anyone," Nancy said. "Not even George."

Kate nodded. She peered at Nancy through her dark lashes. "What else do you know?" she asked.

Nancy hesitated. She didn't want to betray Mr. Garrison's confidence, but she decided to use the information to draw Kate out. Finally Nancy said, "That you have some of the same sort of money problems as Ellen Sedgewick."

Kate stared at her. "Well put, Nancy," she said sharply. "I hope you don't think I had something to do with that theft."

Nancy was surprised at how direct Kate was. Clearly this coach believed that the best defense was a good offense.

"I don't know enough about the case to think anything right now," she said.

Kate leaned back. "Well, that's something. But

I'm not at all happy that you know about my quitting, or about my money problems, either. The only person who could have told you about them is Russell Garrison, and he's not one of my favorite people."

"Why not?"

"I've always felt he was very selfish," Kate said. "I think he doesn't really care as much about Pineview as he says. Don't ask me why I think that. It's just a feeling."

"How about you? Once the girls learn you're leaving, they're going to wonder about your loyalty."

"My reasons for quitting are personal," Kate said. "I don't have a choice. Let's leave it at that, all right?"

Before Nancy could reply, George burst into the room. She looked very upset. "Coach!" she said as she rushed to join them. "More bad news. Some of our equipment is missing!"

Kate stood up. "What's gone?" she asked.

"A couple of balls, Janine's knee pads, one of the equipment bags, and who knows what else? I didn't stay to look through everything."

"Great," Kate said in disgust. "And we've got a game tomorrow." She sighed. "All right, practice is going to be short. When it's over, we'll go back and check again."

The team's luck had certainly turned bad. Halfway through practice, one of the girls began dribbling the ball in on Janine's goal. Janine came

46

out to cut down the angle on the shot. But instead of shooting, the girl continued to dribble and ran smack into Janine. The two girls fell with a thud. Janine lay gasping for breath.

Kate, George, and Nancy ran onto the field. The other girl, Leslie Phillips, looked at Kate. "Sorry, Coach. I wanted to try to fake around her, but I guess I lost control."

"This was a light shooting drill, Leslie," said Kate. "You're not supposed to carry the ball in that deep. Next time, listen to me."

Janine seemed to be recovering. She had had the wind knocked out of her. George and Nancy helped her to her feet, but she was still dizzy.

"Are you all right?" Kate asked.

"I think so," Janine answered. "A little wobbly."

"Better go take a shower and relax. We're almost finished, anyway. We don't need any more dumb accidents."

Janine started toward the gym. After a few steps, she turned back toward the coach.

"Do you really think that was an accident, Coach?"

Kate just shook her head. Then she whistled the girls down to the far end of the field.

"What did Janine mean by that?" Nancy asked George.

"I'm not sure. But Leslie Phillips is Kelly Lewis's best friend."

Nancy thought about her conversation with

Kelly. The girl certainly had it in for Janine. She hesitated before telling George about her conversation, though. She didn't want to gossip about one of the team members. Still, George might have an opinion.

"Kelly really wishes she could play goalie for the tournament," she said to George.

George snorted. "Don't I know."

Nancy cleared her throat. "You don't think she'd do anything illegal to get a chance to play, do you?"

George turned to stare at her friend. "You mean, like take part in a jewel theft?"

Nancy shrugged. "It's just a thought."

George frowned and looked out at the girls, who stood in a circle around Coach Boggs. "Kelly's a pretty determined girl," George said. "I wouldn't put very much past her. But still . . ."

Nancy patted her friend's arm. "We'll talk about it later," she said.

After practice, George, Kate, and Nancy looked for Janine, but she had already gone back to her room. Kate and George decided to go through the equipment to see whether anything else was missing. Nancy decided to tag along. George was still wondering out loud how the equipment could have disappeared when Kate suddenly said, "Is this what you're looking for?"

She held up Janine's knee pads. George stared in disbelief. Then Kate pointed to the far corner, where the missing equipment bag and a few other things sat.

"Open your eyes next time, girl," she said.

George shook her head. She went over and looked at the equipment.

Then she turned to look Nancy squarely in the eye.

"I *swear* that stuff was missing the first time I came down here," she said. "No one can tell me otherwise."

6

Strange Behavior

"I'm sure the equipment wasn't there before!" George insisted again after Coach Boggs had left to go home.

Nancy nodded slowly. "I believe you," she said. "Too many things are happening at once around here. The question is, how and why are they happening? And do any of these problems with the soccer team have something to do with the jewel theft?"

She and George talked about the possibility as they left the gym and sat on the stone steps outside. Nancy wanted to tell George what she'd learned about Kate Boggs, especially that the popular coach had a strong motive for stealing the jewels. But she had promised Kate and the headmaster to keep confidential the coach's money problems.

Besides, George didn't seem nearly as concerned about the jewel theft as she did about the team's recent bad luck.

"I give up," George said at last. "We're never going to figure out what's going on here. Let's go home."

"All right," Nancy agreed. But she didn't really want to leave. She had a strong feeling that the answer to everything was right there at Pineview—maybe right under her nose. But the pieces of the puzzle were still as scattered as the autumn leaves that drifted in every direction.

Just as George and Nancy stood up to leave, Nancy saw a large car pull into the parking lot next to the gym. A woman got out.

"Isn't that Ellen Sedgewick?" Nancy asked.

"Looks like her," George answered.

"I wonder what she's doing here?"

"Visiting Janine, probably."

"But she's headed toward the administration building, not the dormitory."

George nodded. "You're right."

"You can go home if you want to," Nancy said, "but I want to see Mr. Garrison. And I think I'll have a talk with Mrs. Sedgewick. I want to hear her side of the story firsthand."

"I can't go home. I don't have my car. Bess dropped me off this morning. Tell you what.

51

While you do that, I'll go back down to the equipment room. I want to double-check that everything's there. I'm going to make my own list in case equipment goes missing again."

"Good idea."

George headed back to the gym. Nancy ran across the campus to the administration building.

"Mrs. Sedgewick," she called. "May I speak with you?"

Janine's mother stopped on the sidewalk and waited. She looked unsure of who Nancy was.

"Sorry to shout," Nancy said as she reached the older woman. "I just wanted to speak with you for a minute. I'm Nancy Drew."

"Oh, yes. Carson's daughter." Mrs. Sedgewick gave Nancy a tired smile. She looked as if she hadn't been sleeping well. "Janine told me you're some kind of detective and that you're looking into the theft. Frankly, I don't see what you can do to untangle this whole mess. Why is it when things go bad, they always seem to get worse?"

Nancy was touched by Mrs. Sedgewick's sad smile. She felt a rush of sympathy for her.

"Have the police talked to you yet?"

"Several times. I expect they'll arrest me any minute now."

"They can't do that without evidence. And this case seems strangely lacking in evidence."

"I still can't understand it." Mrs. Sedgewick sighed and shook her head. "Those brooches are very valuable, but who at Pineview or in the community here would do such a thing?"

"Someone who also knew the value of the jewels?"

Mrs. Sedgewick looked at Nancy sharply. "Everyone knew after Mr. Ray examined them that morning."

"Ah, but the thief, or thieves, would have had to plan this long before. Remember, they needed time to make perfect copies of the brooches."

"I've thought and thought," the older woman said. "And I just can't figure it out."

"Tell me this," Nancy said. "Were there many people who knew about the brooches before you decided to donate them to Pineview?"

"Not really. I never wore them. They were always in the vault. Some people in my family knew. But no one who would have a reason to steal them."

"So you think it's someone connected with Pineview?"

"I hate to think that," Mrs. Sedgewick said. "I went here myself when I was young. I had some wonderful teachers."

"Like Mr. Morse?"

"Oh, yes. In fact, Jonathan Morse was a good friend of my father's. He often came to our house to dine."

"I met Mr. Morse this morning," Nancy said. "I really liked him."

Ellen Sedgewick smiled. "He's an excellent artist, too. He can paint, sculpt, and do wonderful sketches. I always said if he hadn't been so dedicated to his students, he could have gone very far in the art world."

"Well, we all have to make choices," Nancy said. "I'm sure thousands of Pineview girls are glad Mr. Morse chose as he did."

"You're very perceptive, young lady."

"By the way, may I ask why you've come here today?" Nancy said.

"I'm going to see Russell Garrison. I have an awful feeling he thinks I had something to do with the robbery. I just want to convince him I didn't."

"That might not be a good idea," Nancy said. She sounded almost stern.

"Why not?" asked Mrs. Sedgewick.

"Because you haven't been accused of anything. If you talk too much about being innocent, people might start suspecting that you really *do* have something to hide. The best thing for you and Janine to do is to wait until the real thief is caught."

"Maybe you're right, Nancy. All right, I'll follow your advice. I just hope someone finds the culprit soon. This whole thing really has me worried. But I won't pay a visit to Russell."

"I will," said Nancy. "And I'll let you know how things are going."

Mrs. Sedgewick got back into her car and

54

pulled out of the lot. Nancy watched her go. Once the car was out of sight, Nancy went inside the administration building and headed for Russell Garrison's office.

The hallway was deserted. Most of the staff had already gone home for the day. As Nancy approached Russell Garrison's office, she heard loud voices. Two people were arguing. Nancy walked closer. She strained to hear what the voices inside the office were saying.

"That's not fair," the first voice shouted. "I shouldn't have to do that. You told me before that you would take care of everything!"

The second voice replied, but it was too quiet to make out the words.

"I'm warning you, Garrison. Don't cross me. You're no institution here. There are some people who wouldn't mind seeing you go, too."

The office door was flung open, and Jonathan Morse came charging out. He was so angry that he didn't even see Nancy at first. He ran smack into her.

This time, though, he didn't stop. His face was beet red with rage. He brushed right past Nancy and continued down the hallway.

Very curious, Nancy knocked on the headmaster's open door.

Garrison had his back to the door. He didn't see who was knocking. "Jonathan, I refuse to discuss this further," he said over his shoulder. "You'll do as you're told or I'll—"

He turned to see Nancy standing in the doorway. His mouth dropped open for a moment with surprise and annoyance. Then he forced a smile.

"Why, Ms. Drew. I wasn't expecting you. But then, I guess this is how detectives work. Doing the unexpected. Come in, please."

Nancy entered the office. Before she could say anything, Garrison spoke again.

"I've just had a very distressing talk with Mr. Morse," he said. "You remember him. It seems that some of our trustees are worried about his age. They'd like to see him retire. I told him I would do everything I could to let him stay and teach. But the way he was just now—upset and nearly out of control—I'm not so sure the trustees are wrong."

Nancy marveled at how calm Mr. Garrison could appear so soon after such a big argument. She wondered whether he was telling the truth.

"I thought Mr. Morse was one of the school's favorite teachers," she said.

"He is. But sometimes I wonder. After all, he is in his seventies. Maybe the girls just think of him as a grandfatherly type."

That wasn't how Ellen Sedgewick had described him. And just a few hours before, Mr. Garrison himself had told Nancy how valuable Mr. Morse was.

"We really should have a definite retirement age," Mr. Garrison continued. "That would keep this from becoming such a problem. In fact, I think I'll bring that up at the next meeting. Now, what can I do for you, Ms. Drew?"

"I have some questions about the robbery," Nancy said.

"More unpleasantness." Mr. Garrison sighed. "This hasn't been a very good few days."

"I was wondering whether you'd remembered anything since our last talk. Maybe there was someone else who could have gotten to the jewels between the morning examination and the auction."

"I told you everything I knew last time." He sounded a little annoyed. "The same things I told the police."

"I'm sure you did," Nancy said. "But tell me something else. How important to the school is this Canadian Cup soccer tournament?"

Garrison seemed surprised by the question. "What does that have to do with the jewel theft?" he asked.

"I don't know," Nancy admitted. "But the auction was supposed to help the soccer team. I've noticed some problems at practice. I was just curious."

Garrison shrugged. "Of course, winning the cup would be a feather in our cap," he said. "But Pineview can do just fine without it. We don't really specialize in athletics."

Nancy nodded. "Well, it's getting late," she said. "Thanks for seeing me."

"You're welcome." Mr. Garrison smiled at her. "Actually, this has been the easiest part of my day."

"I understand." Nancy shook his hand and turned to leave. As she did, Mr. Garrison called her back.

"Wait a minute, Ms. Drew. I have one question of my own," he said.

"Yes?"

Garrison hesitated. He seemed unsure whether to go on. "Have you been able to use the information I gave you about Coach Boggs? She still owes us that money, you see."

"I've talked to her," Nancy said carefully. "But she didn't tell me much that I didn't already know."

Garrison nodded. He looked down at his hands. "Not that I want to spread gossip about her," he said. "I should explain that Ms. Boggs and I have never really gotten along. It's just that I have this feeling about her. . . ."

Nancy nodded. The headmaster was acting awfully strange. "Thank you, Mr. Garrison," she said. "I'll keep my eyes open."

"Oh, Ms. Drew? May I remind you that what I told you about her is just between us?"

"I'll remember. Thanks again."

As Nancy left the administration building she wondered whether George was still in the equipment room. She walked across the lawn to the gym, but the front doors were locked. She went

58

around the building and tried another door. It was open.

Nancy walked through the gloomy gym to the dark metal stairway. She started down, holding on tightly to the rail.

"George?" she called. Her voice echoed against the cement walls. She thought she heard a door open downstairs. She stopped, but there was only silence. Slowly she started down the stairs again.

As she entered the narrow hallway, she heard a low droning sound coming from the room at the end of the hall.

Nancy walked down the corridor to the room. Its large metal door stood partly open. Nancy pushed it open farther and saw, by the light from the corridor, a gigantic boiler pumping heat up into the gym. That was where the droning sound was coming from. Beside the boiler were several large water heaters. The floor of the small room was covered with soot and the walls were black.

Nancy laughed to herself. What had she imagined was down here? But before she could turn around to go back to the equipment room, Nancy heard footsteps behind her. Then two hands shoved her hard from behind. She fell headlong into the boiler room.

"What?" As she started to get up, Nancy heard the large metal door slam shut behind her, then lock.

She was trapped.

7

Trapped!

Nancy leapt up and grabbed the door. She knew it had been locked, but instinct made her try it, anyway. This was certainly no accident.

The door remained shut tight. Nancy felt for the light switch. She couldn't find it. She banged on the heavy door and yelled for help. It was hot in the room with the boiler running. She fought the panicky feeling that there wasn't enough air.

"Help!" she shouted. "Somebody help me!"

No one answered.

"I wonder if I'll be here all night," she said to herself as she sank down to the floor. "By morning I'll have melted away in this heat."

She waited another ten minutes. Then she

stood up and began pounding on the door again, yelling for help. Finally, after what seemed like forever, she heard someone pound back.

"Nancy, is that you?"

"George!"

"Hang on, Nan. I'll be right back."

Nancy wiped the perspiration from her face and waited. Finally she heard the sound of a key in the lock. The big heavy door swung open. The light rushed in faster than George, but her friend wasn't far behind. Behind George stood a big, burly man dressed in jeans and a dirty T-shirt.

"What happened, Nan? Are you all right? When you didn't come down to meet me I went over to Mr. Garrison's office. He said you'd left, so I came back here. I figured you might have gotten lost."

" 'Lost' isn't the word. Someone shoved me in here and locked the door."

"Are you kidding?" George stared at her, wide-eyed.

"Do I look as if I'm kidding? It's hot and dirty in here!"

"That's why we leave the door open, ma'am," the burly man said.

"This is Mr. Quinn, the custodian," George said. "He had the key."

Nancy turned to him. "Thanks for helping, Mr. Quinn."

The custodian nodded. Nancy looked at

George. "Come on. I need air." The two of them walked outside and sat on the front steps.

"This is where we came in," George said.

"But a lot has changed in the last hour, George. For the first time since I've been on this case, someone has let me know he—or she—doesn't like it. Thanks for coming to the rescue. I was beginning to wonder if . . ." She stopped and looked over George's shoulder.

George followed her gaze. Kate Boggs was coming out of the gym. She waved and walked over to them.

"I thought you girls had gone home," she said.

"We thought you had, too," George replied. "We had a little accident here."

"Oh, no. What now?"

"Nancy got locked in the boiler room," George said before Nancy could stop her.

"She what?"

Nancy sighed. "Someone shoved me into the boiler room and locked the door," she said.

"Why would anyone do that?" exclaimed Kate.

"I think it had to do with my investigating the jewel theft," said Nancy.

"When did this happen?"

"About half an hour ago."

"I didn't hear anything," Kate said.

"You were in the gym then?" George asked. "I didn't see you."

"I went to the lockers to see which girls had picked up their uniforms for tomorrow's game. Then I went to the equipment room."

"That's where I was," George said. "Until I started looking for Nancy."

"We must have just missed each other." Kate looked off toward the parking lot.

Nancy decided to change the subject. "So is the team ready for the Forsythe game, Kate?" she asked.

"Not really. If we were playing a tougher team I'd be worried. Janine is almost a basket case. And Kelly Lewis seems more concerned with Janine than with her own playing. I was planning to start Kelly tomorrow, but now I'm not sure. But I'm sure of this much. If Janine doesn't straighten out soon, we don't have much chance to win the Canadian Cup."

The three of them walked to the parking lot together. George and Nancy got into Nancy's car and headed back toward River Heights.

"What a day," Nancy said. "More leads than I can handle, but not one that makes sense. By the way, are you sure you didn't know Kate was in the gym?"

"Of course not," George answered. "Nan, you don't think Kate locked you in the boiler room, do you?"

Nancy shook her head. "I don't know what to think."

"Kate! That really takes the cake. As if she didn't have enough problems with the team!"

George was annoyed that Nancy could even hint at Kate Boggs's doing anything so mean. Nancy could sense that. But she couldn't tell her friend what she knew about Kate's money problems and the fact that she was quitting her job at Pineview.

Nancy kept quiet the rest of the way to George's house. After dropping George off, she drove home.

"Nancy, what happened to you!" said Hannah Gruen as soon as Nancy walked in the door.

"Would you believe I got locked in a boiler room, Hannah?" Nancy said with a grin.

"Knowing you, I'd believe anything," the older woman retorted.

"Well, the good news is, I got out," Nancy said.

"So I see. Your father will be home soon. Why don't you get cleaned up before he sees you?"

"I will, Hannah. I just have to make one phone call first."

The call was to Chicago. Nancy had decided to place it on her way home from George's. She dialed Information first. Then she called the number and was soon connected and listening to a man's voice on the other end.

"This is Gideon Ray. What can I do for you?"

"Mr. Ray, my name is Nancy Drew. I'm looking into the jewel theft at Pineview School. May I ask you a couple of questions?"

"I've told the police everything I know. I hope you people don't think I had anything to do with the theft."

"No one thinks you were a part of it, Mr. Ray," said Nancy. She tried to sound as harmless as possible. "I'm a private detective working for the Sedgewick family. May I ask you a few quick questions?"

There was a long pause on the other end of the line. Finally, Gideon Ray said, "All right. But please make it brief."

"Thank you, Mr. Ray. Could you tell me when you first saw the two brooches?"

"The morning of the auction."

"And you were sure these brooches were real antiques?" Nancy asked.

"Definitely. Fine-quality stones. Very valuable pieces."

Nancy made a note in her small notebook. "Who hired you to do the appraisal?" she asked.

"I was paid by the school. Mr. Garrison said he wanted to hold the auction in a professional way, since the money would go to Pineview."

"Of course. And that's why you examined the jewels a second time?"

"No. I was simply to write down my earlier appraisal and seal it in the envelope. For drama, you know. But at the last minute I thought it would make a better show if I actually examined the jewels again, in front of everyone."

"So no one knew you were going to do that?"

"It was my own idea." Mr. Ray said. "And if I hadn't reexamined the brooches, no one would ever have known about the theft. Some bidder would have spent a hundred thousand dollars on two lumps of paste, you and I wouldn't be having this conversation, and I'd be happily on my way home to dinner now."

8

Where's Kelly?

Nancy lay in bed a long time that night, just thinking. She had several suspects to think about now. There was Mrs. Sedgewick—not a very likely one, of course. Kate Boggs had a strong motive, and she had been in the gym when Nancy was locked inside the boiler room. Kelly Lewis wasn't near the jewels as far as Nancy knew, but she still had to be considered, because of her resentment toward Janine. And now that Mr. Ray had said no one knew he was going to reexamine the jewels, Mr. Garrison and all the others involved in the auction were suspects, too.

Nancy didn't know whom to suspect most. She did know that time was growing short. Whoever had switched the jewels wasn't going to sit on them for very long. The brooches would have to be moved out of River Heights, the sooner the better. Nancy felt that somehow all the threads of the puzzle were there, but she still wasn't close to tying them together.

Nancy woke up early the next morning, even though she hadn't had much sleep. George had invited her to ride with the team to the Forsythe School game, and Nancy wanted to be there. She looked forward to keeping an eye on Coach Boggs and Kelly Lewis. She was also concerned about how well Janine was holding up.

She arrived at the school at nine-thirty. George would be there by ten o'clock, and Bess was coming with her. Nancy wanted to do a little sleuthing before her friends arrived.

She walked over to Braithwaite Hall, where many of the classrooms were located. Fortunately, the man she was looking for was already there.

"Mr. Morse, may I speak with you a minute?"

Morse looked up from the worktable in his art classroom. "Oh, yes. You're Ms. Drew. I remember you well."

Nancy smiled. The lovable and charming old teacher was back. But she hadn't come for chit-chat. This time she meant to ask questions.

"I'm glad you're looking better today, Mr. Morse," she said.

"Thank you. But when did I look so bad?"

"When I saw you coming out of Mr. Garrison's office yesterday."

The expression on the old man's face went sour in a flash. He began puttering around his worktable. The table was cluttered with all kinds of art materials—paints and sculpting tools—as well as with student projects.

"I hope nothing is seriously wrong," Nancy continued. "If there is, maybe I can help."

"Help? You aren't on the board of trustees by any chance, are you, young lady?"

"I'm afraid not. When I was outside Mr. Garrison's office, I heard you arguing. In fact, it sounded as if you were, well, threatening him."

The teacher's eyes opened wide. "Me threaten Russell Garrison!" he exclaimed. "Hardly, my dear. He was threatening me!"

"In what way?"

"With my life! Or practically, that is. He wants to kick me out of this place."

"He did say he thought you should retire," Nancy admitted.

Jonathan Morse looked at her for a moment. "Ms. Drew," he said. "Every headmaster since I've been here has told me that I would remain a part of Pineview for as long as I am able to teach. Ask any of my students right now, today, if I can still teach."

"I understand, but—" Nancy began.

"Then Russell Garrison came along," the

69

teacher interrupted. "Ever since he's been in charge I've been under the gun. I know he's telling the board I'm too old. But it's not true! I'm just as capable as I always was. Plus, I have experience!"

Nancy cleared her throat. "Mr. Morse, do you think Mr. Garrison has something personal against you?"

The teacher shut his mouth and stared at her. Then he looked away. "Certainly not." He fumbled with his art supplies. "And besides, I shouldn't discuss these matters."

"I'm only trying to help."

"That's very kind of you, young lady. But everything's taken care of. Um, by the way, are you going to the soccer game?"

"Why, yes, I am."

"You tell those girls to win it," he said fiercely. "I'd like to see one Canadian Cup in the trophy case here at Pineview before I go."

Nancy left, feeling sorry for the old man. But she couldn't help wondering whether there was something more between the art teacher and Mr. Garrison than they were telling her. Mr. Morse's anger yesterday in the headmaster's office had been so great. Even the suggestion of retirement didn't seem enough to spark it.

"But then, I don't know Mr. Morse," Nancy reminded herself. "At least, not very well."

* * *

When Nancy reached the parking lot outside the gym, George and Bess were already there. A few team members were kicking a ball around on the pavement.

"Well, well," Nancy said. "Don't tell me Bess Marvin is going to attend a soccer game."

"I talked her into it," said George. "I told her if she didn't come I'd never go to another rock concert with her."

"Blackmailer," said Bess. "Your team had better win."

"With George coaching, how can they lose?" Nancy asked.

"I was telling Bess about all the fun she missed yesterday," George said.

"If you call getting shoved into a boiler room fun," Nancy replied.

"Depends on who's in there with you," Bess said, her eyes twinkling.

By now more members of the team had arrived. Finally, Kate Boggs arrived. The coach looked tired and drawn, and she seemed upset. She walked straight into the gym without waving to George or talking to any of the players.

"I wonder what's wrong with her," George said.

"Maybe she just feels the pressure," said Nancy.

"I'll go help her get ready for the trip," George said.

After George had run off, Bess asked, "What's going on around here?"

"That's what I'm trying to find out," said Nancy. "But it hasn't been easy."

When Janine arrived a few minutes later, she walked toward the group, wearing the same downcast look as her coach. It seemed as though no one at Pineview was happy.

"Have you found anything out yet?" Janine asked Nancy as soon as she reached her.

"Nothing definite, but I'm working on it," Nancy said.

"My mother is a nervous wreck," Janine said. "The insurance company told her they're hiring their own detective. They said they won't pay the claim until she's been cleared."

"She's just got to hang in there a little longer," Nancy said. "This will all work out."

"Maybe," Janine said. "But meanwhile it's really getting to me. I almost didn't come today. I don't feel like playing. Kelly's starting as goalie, and for all I care, she can have her dream come true and play the whole game."

A couple of the other girls called to Janine to join them. Obviously they hoped to cheer her up.

Nancy watched some players pass the soccer ball, working up their spirit for the game. George and Kate returned from the gym, and Kate told the girls to get their equipment bags from downstairs. Before letting them go, she took a head count. Someone was missing.

"It's Kelly," one of the girls shouted. "She's not here."

"Where is she?" said Coach Boggs. "Kelly's never missed a game before."

"I'll call her dorm," Leslie Phillips volunteered. She ran inside the gym to use the phone.

"It figures," Nancy heard Janine mutter. "The one day I don't want to play, she's not here."

Leslie returned from the gym, out of breath from running. "Kelly's not at the dorm," she panted. "She must be on her way here."

"We can wait another fifteen minutes, that's all," Kate said.

The time passed quickly as the girls gathered their gym bags and boarded the bus. When everyone was ready, Kelly had still not appeared.

"We have to leave," Kate announced. "We can't miss the game because of one player."

The bus pulled out of the parking lot. Mr. Quinn, the custodian, was driving. Some of the girls looked out the back windows for Kelly, but she was nowhere in sight.

Nancy sat in the front seat next to Kate. George and Bess sat across the aisle, one row back. As the bus headed out onto the highway, Nancy asked Kate how things were going.

"Not great. I'm waiting to hear about something that could solve one of my problems. But then there's still another one."

"Anything you want to talk about?"

Kate turned her sharp eyes on Nancy. "Look, I

know you mean well," she said. "But I guess I'm just a private person. I don't like to make my problems someone else's problems. I'll handle it."

"By quitting?" Nancy said in a low voice.

"That's just part of it."

"Does that part have anything to do with Mr. Garrison?"

Kate frowned suspiciously. "Why do you ask that?"

"Well, he seems to have a finger in everything that goes on at Pineview. I know Mr. Morse is having problems with him."

Nancy was careful not to tell Kate what Mr. Morse's problem was.

"Jonathan is such a wonderful teacher," Kate said. She hesitated and then went on. "It's true, Russell Garrison and I don't always see eye to eye. But he has supported the soccer program."

"He claims he's helped you out in other ways, too." Nancy thought of the money Kate had borrowed from the school.

"Let me tell you something about Russell Garrison," Kate said. "He never does anyone a favor without asking for something in return. That's all I have to say."

The bus continued down the main highway for more than an hour. Nancy dozed off a couple of times. The second time she awakened to find that the bus was traveling on an old two-lane country road.

74

"Where are we?" she asked sleepily.

"Route Twenty-seven," said Kate. "About ten miles outside of Crighton, where the Forsythe School is."

Just then Nancy saw a barrier across the road and a detour sign pointing to the right. Mr. Quinn swung the bus onto an even narrower, bumpier road that was full of potholes.

Kate leaned forward.

"What's going on?" she asked Mr. Quinn.

"Road construction, I guess. This should take us back to Twenty-seven."

The old bus half rolled and half bounced downhill on the gravel trail. It was traveling pretty fast when the road took a sudden left turn. Nancy noticed a small sign that read Baxter's Creek. Mr. Quinn pumped the brakes as they went around the curve.

Then he shouted, "Oh, no!"

Nancy sat up and looked out the windshield. About fifty yards in front of them were barriers across the road. A huge sign said Bridge Out.

"I don't think I can stop!" Mr. Quinn yelled.

"We're going to crash!" shrieked Bess.

The girls screamed as the bus skidded toward the barriers that guarded the missing bridge.

9

Hustle and High Fives

For the next few seconds there was noise everywhere. The squeal of brakes, the sound of tires skidding on the road, and the screams of almost every girl on the bus. Mr. Quinn's knuckles were white on the steering wheel.

But he stopped the bus! It knocked over the first barrier. Then it came to a halt about five feet from where the road ended and dropped off into the creek a hundred feet below.

For a moment there was silence. Then a couple of the girls began to cry. Nancy breathed a sigh of relief. She looked back at her friends. Bess was ashen. George was wiping off her face with a tissue.

Kate got up quickly and made sure the girls were all right. Nancy, meanwhile, got out of the bus and saw how close they had come to a tragic accident. Then she saw a police car come flying up the road behind them. A young trooper got out quickly.

"Everyone all right here?" he asked Nancy.

"I think so," Nancy said. "But we're all pretty shaken up."

"Can't blame you," said the trooper. "Not a very funny joke, if that's what it was. If we get the guy who did this, there will be some serious charges. I can promise you that."

"A joke?" asked Nancy. She looked at Kate, Bess, and George, who had climbed off the bus and were joining her.

"Someone changed the road signs back there. This was the road that was closed. A guy who lives up the road saw the bus turn down here and called us. I guess we're going to have to keep a better eye on things around here. Are you folks sure you're all right?"

"Yes. But we've still got a soccer game to play," Kate said.

As the others climbed back into the bus, Bess tugged on Nancy's arm and pulled her a little to one side. "What do you think about all this?" she asked in a low voice.

"I sure don't like it," replied Nancy. "We could have been killed. I mean, you can't help wondering whether someone switched the signs on purpose."

"Exactly! And where was Kelly Lewis?" Bess

whispered. "Why would she not show up for this game and this game only?"

Nancy shook her head. "I don't know, Bess, but I intend to find out."

By the time the bus arrived at Forsythe School, it was almost game time. The girls dressed quickly and then ran out onto the field for warm-ups. Nancy's mind was full of questions, and Bess was still nervous from the near-crash. But once the game started they both relaxed a bit and enjoyed the action.

The Forsythe players weren't very good, but at first they looked like world champs compared to Pineview. Maybe Pineview School's poor play was caused by the accident with the bus. Or it might have arisen out of the conflict between Janine and Kelly. In any case, Pineview looked like anything but Canadian Cup contenders.

In the first minute of play, a pair of Forsythe forwards broke into the attacking zone. Leslie Phillips was playing fullback, but when she started to cut for the ball, she fell down. The Forsythe forward took a shot from about twenty feet away. It was the kind of shot Janine usually stopped with ease. Only this time she bent down a split second too late. The ball skidded past her for a score.

"Come on, Janine, look alive out there!" George yelled. Minutes later, Forsythe scored a second point when Janine let another shot slip past her into the net.

By now George was running up and down the sideline, encouraging the girls. But Kate did next to nothing. She sat, strangely quiet, on the players' bench.

"George really puts on a show out there," Bess said to Nancy. "Watching her is worth the price of admission."

"Right now she probably wishes she could go out there and play," said Nancy.

Gradually the Pineview team started to come alive. In the closing seconds of the half, they finally scored, cutting the Forsythe lead to 2–1. The girls seemed a little more spirited as they came off the field, but Kate was very rough on them.

"I don't know what's happening to you, girls. I see selfishness out there. A lack of teamwork. You're not the same team I coached at the beginning of the season. If you play this way in Canada, Pineview will be the laughingstock of the competition."

Some of the girls looked at each other. A few nodded in agreement. Others acted as if they didn't care.

"Well, if you girls don't care," Kate continued, "I don't, either. Do whatever you want out there during the second half. I'm going back to the bus."

With that, Kate left the circle of players and walked across the field to the bus. The girls were stunned as they watched their coach leave. No one uttered a sound. Finally, George walked to the center of the circle. She looked around at the downcast group. The Forsythe team was already coming back onto the field.

"Are we going to blow a whole season because no one feels like playing?" George yelled. "Or because we've got other things on our minds? Apparently Coach Boggs thinks we are. How about proving her wrong? Any athlete worth her salt knows that no game is easy. But she also knows she has to put her personal feelings aside. She has to go out and play her best."

The girls looked at George. They were listening carefully. George smiled at them. "I want to see some tough defense," she said. "Crisp passing. And good shots. Let's show them why Pineview is going to win the Canadian Cup!"

George's pep talk seemed to light a fire under the girls. They jumped to their feet, screaming, "Go! Go! Go! Go!" all together. The starters took the field.

Janine walked slowly toward the goal. One of the other girls ran past, put a hand on her shoulder, and said, "Come on, Janine, let's see a little hustle."

Janine raised her head and broke into a brisk

trot to the goal. She smoothed out a small dirt area in front of the net and finally looked ready. Shortly after the start of the period, she made a beautiful diving save to her right, grabbing the hard shot in midair. She landed with a thud, but bounced right back up and booted the ball half the length of the field.

A teammate caught the ball and headed it toward the opposite goal. A Pineview halfback picked it up and passed it to a forward who tied the game with a hard shot into the right-hand corner of the Forsythe net.

To their credit, Forsythe didn't give up. The game stayed tied until the final two minutes, but the battling Forsythe team wouldn't quit. When one of their forwards got past Leslie Phillips and came in on goal alone, it looked as if they might get the winning tally. But Janine took three quick steps to her left. She dived to the ground and just managed to get her fingertips on the ball to knock it away. Then she leapt to her feet and again threw herself on the loose ball before a Forsythe player could reach it.

Janine had made a brilliant save. She quickly threw the ball up the middle to one of her halfbacks. Another quick pass and Paula LeGere had the ball again on the right side. She launched a centering pass to about forty feet in front of the goal.

Celia Warren settled the ball after one bounce.

She made a perfect pass to Denise Rogers. Denise took the pass and blasted the winning score into the left corner of the net.

Pineview had won the game, 4–3. But they'd made what should have been an easy game into a fierce struggle for survival.

Clinching a spot in the Canadian Cup Tournament seemed to change the team's mood completely. There was shouting and singing on the way back to Pineview School. The moodiness of the earlier trip and the near-accident were almost forgotten. The only unhappy person on the bus was Kate Boggs.

"I let them down," she said to Nancy. "I let my own feelings get in the way of my coaching. I've never done that before. That only proves that getting out is the right decision after all. If George hadn't talked to them the way she did, I don't know if they would have come back."

"Don't be so hard on yourself," said Nancy. "It's been a rough few days for everyone."

"It's been more than a few days," Kate said. "I know we all make mistakes, but some of us regret them more than others."

Nancy looked at the coach, confused. Was Kate Boggs admitting to something? It was impossible to tell.

When the bus rolled into the Pineview parking lot there were banners everywhere:

Canadian Cup Champs

Good Luck in Canada

Let's Win the Big One

The Cup or Bust

It looked as if the entire school had gathered to meet the team. The students had prepared a surprise victory party in the gym. There were refreshments, a sound system blaring rock music, and a huge poster with all the scores from the season's games. As the girls jumped off the bus, they grinned and shook their index fingers in the air, the traditional sign meaning, "We're number one!" The teachers and students clapped and cheered. The school was certainly behind its soccer team.

The team members' faces shone as they entered the gym. "All right!" one of them shouted to the others. "Let's party!"

Suddenly Kelly Lewis appeared in the doorway. She wasn't smiling. She hesitated, like an unwanted guest waiting to be invited inside. As the girls noticed Kelly standing there, the mood of the party started to swing down once again.

Leslie Phillips was the first to go up to Kelly. "What happened to you?" she asked her friend.

"I missed the bus," Kelly said. "I'm sorry. But I'm glad you guys won."

Several other girls walked up to Kelly. They pulled her into the gym. But it was obvious that tension was in the air once more.

Nancy looked over at Janine. She'd been happy coming back on the bus. Now she was no longer smiling. She seemed to be shrinking away from everyone.

Before anyone else could say anything, Kate Boggs reappeared. She had been down in the equipment room. She saw Kelly across the gym floor and gave her a cold stare. Then she walked quickly toward her.

"Young lady," Kate said, "you owe us all an explanation. And it had better be good."

"I missed the bus," Kelly repeated. "I'm sorry."

"'I'm sorry,' isn't good enough," Kate snapped. Her voice echoed in the suddenly quiet gym. "You let this team down. One of the most important games we've ever had and you missed the bus. I want to know why."

Kelly look at her coach. She was on the verge of tears.

"Come on, young lady, we're all waiting," Kate repeated.

The other girls drew closer around Kate and Kelly. Everyone waited for an answer.

Kelly shuffled her feet and took a deep breath.

She looked at the girls nearest to her, then looked beyond them. She seemed to be looking for something, or somebody, to save her.

"There's the reason I missed the game," she said, pointing beyond the circle of girls. "It was because of her!"

Everyone turned and looked. Kelly was pointing straight at Janine Sedgewick.

10

A Team in Trouble

All heads turned to look at Janine. She instinctively took a few steps back, as though she were guilty of something. But this time the coach would hear none of it.

"Kelly, how in the world could it be Janine's fault that you missed the bus?"

"I—I'm not supposed to tell," the girl stammered.

"I think you'd better. This is a serious accusation."

Kelly stared at the floor. "Mr. Garrison called me to his office to ask me some questions about the Sedgewicks," she admitted at last.

Nancy stepped forward immediately. "What kind of questions?" she demanded.

"He asked about Janine. Whether she had talked about the jewel theft."

Kelly stopped and looked around. "He thought maybe Janine had said something. Anything that might make her seem guilty."

"You mean he suspects Janine of stealing the brooches?" said George. "I don't believe it."

"I'm just telling you what the headmaster said," Kelly answered. She relaxed a little now that everyone was listening attentively. "And he kept me for so long that by the time I got out I'd missed the bus."

While Kelly talked, no one noticed Janine backing away toward the far end of the gym. Suddenly a loud sob broke across the room.

"Janine!" George called.

It was too late. Janine had run crying from the gym. George ran after her. A satisfied smirk flitted across Kelly's lips. But it disappeared in an instant when Coach Boggs turned toward her.

"Now look what you've done," the coach said to Kelly.

"I just explained why I was late."

"Right. And maybe at the same time cost us the Canadian Cup. Just when this team was coming together again, you stepped in and ruined the girls' spirit."

"Don't worry, Coach. If Janine doesn't have the guts to play, I can do the job."

"Oh, really." Kate's face turned red with anger. "Listen, I'm not even sure you're still on the team. And besides, if you can do the job, why haven't you beaten Janine in the past three years? Whether you realize it or not, Kelly, you may have just damaged this team beyond repair. As far as I'm concerned, this party is over. We'll have a light practice tomorrow afternoon to see if we can pick up the pieces. If we can't, I'm afraid our trip to Canada will be a very short one."

Kate turned and stalked out of the gym. Nancy and Bess looked at the girls. Half of them had turned away and were drifting out of the gym. The others rallied around Kelly, clearly siding with her. "If you don't go, I don't go," one of the girls assured Kelly.

"This is not a good situation," Nancy said as she and Bess went outside to look for George.

"What do you think is going to happen?"

"I don't know. What I do know is that I've got to find some answers, and fast."

They spotted George walking back from the administration building.

"Janine ran in there, called her mother, and wouldn't even talk to me," George said. "We've got a real problem."

"That's for sure," Nancy said. "And 'we' is right. The team has a problem, and so do I. It's time I did something about it."

"Like what?" asked Bess.

Nancy frowned. "Like figure out a way to put all these pieces together," she replied.

That night Nancy decided to call the Crighton Police Department. A Sergeant Parker answered the phone.

"Sergeant, I was on the bus from River Heights that took the wrong turn this morning."

"Oh, yes. The one that almost went into Baxter's Creek. You were very lucky."

"I'm curious whether you know who switched those road signs."

"As a matter of fact, we do. They were moved by the Bullock brothers. They're a couple of local wiseguys. An elderly woman who lives near that turnoff saw two men acting suspiciously this morning. She got a partial license plate number on the car, and we traced it to the Bullocks. They've done stuff like this before. This time they'll be cooling their heels in jail for a while."

"You're sure about that, Sergeant? This is very important."

"I got it right from the horse's mouth. The Bullocks admitted it. So this case is closed."

Nancy wished her case were closed as well. She thanked Sergeant Parker and hung up.

So it looked as if the near-accident had nothing to do with Nancy's investigation. But the Kelly-Janine connection still bothered her. And why was Mr. Garrison asking questions about the

Sedgewicks? She needed answers fast and was determined to get them.

The next morning Nancy drove out to Pineview early and waited for Jonathan Morse to arrive at his classroom. The old teacher smiled when he saw her.

"Why do we keep meeting like this, my dear?" he quipped.

"I have a few questions I'd like to ask, if you have some time to talk. Can we speak in your classroom?" Nancy asked.

"Certainly."

He smiled as he opened his classroom door. Nancy followed him inside. The room was a mess, as usual. The teacher kept his students doing so many different things that he never had time to clean.

"Mr. Morse, you know about Mrs. Sedgewick's brooches being stolen, don't you?"

"Everyone at Pineview knows about that."

"You're a sculptor. How hard would it be for someone to make copies of those brooches? Copies so well made that only an expert could tell the difference?"

The teacher frowned and took a deep breath. Nancy looked at him, puzzled.

"I'm a little embarrassed," he explained.

"Embarrassed?"

"I'm supposed to be an art expert. But I know almost nothing about lapidary."

"That's the art of cutting gemstones, right?"

"Very good, my dear. Now, I'd only be guessing, but I would say an expert could easily fashion fake brooches. But I don't know how long it might take him. I'm sure it's very precise and difficult work."

Nancy nodded. "That's what I thought."

"You don't really think someone here at Pineview stole those brooches, do you?" Mr. Morse asked.

"Yes, I do. And I don't think Mrs. Sedgewick had anything to do with it. But I've still got to prove that and find out just who the thief is."

"Can you do that?"

"Not yet. But I won't give up without a fight."

"A detective after my own heart," said the old man. "You make me wish I were fifty years younger. I'd take you out to dinner."

Nancy laughed. "Mr. Morse, you don't have to be fifty years younger to take me to dinner."

"I'll remember that."

Nancy thanked the teacher for his help and left the room. She walked to the end of the hall and bent down to get a drink from the water fountain. That was when she noticed her right hand. "Yuck!" she murmured.

Nancy's hand had traces of a green, greasy substance on it. She must have picked it up in Mr. Morse's room, she decided. She rinsed off her hand under the stream of water, but she couldn't help wondering what the green substance was.

91

First things first, Nancy reminded herself. It was time for another visit with Russell Garrison. This one wouldn't be just small talk, either.

Garrison's secretary wasn't at her desk, so Nancy walked right through the open door to his private office. She found the headmaster reading a stack of folders.

"May I speak with you, Mr. Garrison?"

The headmaster looked up, surprised. "Ms. Drew. I didn't expect to see you again so soon. To tell you the truth I'm rather busy."

"This will take just a few minutes."

Garrison sighed. "Very well. But only a few minutes."

Garrison was barely trying to hide his annoyance. Nancy guessed her next question would annoy him even more.

"All I want to know, Mr. Garrison, is why you keep trying to link Ellen Sedgewick with the jewel theft. Isn't she one of your most generous donors?"

Garrison dropped the folder he was holding and gave Nancy a bewildered look. "What makes you think I'm accusing Mrs. Sedgewick of anything?"

"Mr. Garrison, I know you questioned Kelly Lewis about the Sedgewicks yesterday and caused her to miss the bus to an important soccer game. She blamed Janine, and now the team is being forced to side with either Kelly or Janine."

"I just happened to see Kelly and thought maybe there were some stories going around the soccer team," Mr. Garrison protested. "As for her missing the bus, I have to confess I'd forgotten all about the game. That was my fault."

Nancy could see that the headmaster had his excuses ready. That was the problem with Russell Garrison. He had an excuse for everything.

"Actually," Nancy said, "I've concluded that Mrs. Sedgewick is completely innocent. She had nothing to do with the theft."

"How do you know that?"

"I'm afraid I can't reveal my sources."

Garrison stood up and walked to the window. "Ms. Drew," he said impatiently. "The police are handling this case well enough. I don't see why Pineview needs an amateur detective poking around as well. I'm going to have to ask you to stop this nonsense."

"Let me ask you one more question, then," Nancy said quickly. "Did you know that Mr. Ray would reexamine the brooches at the auction before he wrote down what they were worth? Or did that come as a complete surprise?"

Garrison turned and gave Nancy an angry glare. "Better not play games with me, Ms. Drew. Mr. Ray did an excellent job. I didn't know he was going to examine the jewelry again, but I certainly didn't try to stop him. What are you implying?"

"Relax, Mr. Garrison. I'm just trying to point

out how a case can be made for naming almost anyone as a suspect. No offense intended."

Garrison frowned. "It's not that easy, Ms. Drew. Offense is taken. I'm going to have to ask you to leave. Now. And please keep your hands off this case. If you don't, I'll tell the police to make sure that you do."

Nancy nodded stiffly to the headmaster and left. Clearly she had rattled him, but she still didn't have any idea whether he was involved in the theft. She certainly wouldn't give up on him as a suspect, she decided as she left the administration building. And she was not about to get off the case, no matter what he said.

Nancy met George for lunch, and then went with her friend to soccer practice. The latest incident between Kelly and Janine seemed to have nearly split the team. The girls were standing around in small groups, and a feeling of resentment was in the air.

Janine sat by herself at one end of the field, staring into space. Kelly passed a ball around with Leslie Phillips and some of the other girls. Kate Boggs sat on the bench, looking at a clipboard. She didn't seem interested in starting practice.

"Hi, Coach." George tried to sound cheerful. "Ready to get started?"

"What for?" said Kate. "This isn't a team anymore. Look at them. The biggest games of their lives are just around the corner and they're more concerned with personal problems, like who's going to play goal. I feel like calling the tournament officials and telling them we're not coming."

"Kate!" Nancy said. "Haven't too many people worked too hard for too long to do something like that?"

"Maybe," Kate said. "But I don't know how to beat this."

"Maybe once they start working out they'll come alive," George said.

"Be my guest," said Kate.

George gave a blast of her whistle. She told the girls to jog four easy laps around the field. They all started running, but there was no spirit, no energy. It was a team without a leader. A team in trouble.

When they finished the four laps, George began a couple of light passing drills, including the goalies. Again the girls went through the motions. While George tried to urge them on, Kate stayed on the bench. Nancy stood quietly beside her. No one noticed another spectator at the far end of the field.

The passing drill continued. Even George stopped watching for a minute to join Nancy and Kate. Suddenly a sharp voice rang out.

"You did that on purpose!"

"No way. If you'd been watching, you would have seen the ball coming."

"You weren't supposed to kick it to me, Janine."

"In this game you've got to be ready for anything. You were unprepared, Kelly. Maybe that's why you're only the backup goalie."

Kelly and Janine were at it again. This time they were really shouting at each other. Kate jumped off the bench and sprinted over to the two girls.

"That is enough. I've had it with this squabbling between you two. If either of you can't put the team first, then get out now."

"I'm getting tired of doing what you say," Kelly snapped. "You've never given me a fair chance to win the starting position. A lot of the girls think I should start, and you know it."

"Kelly, we'll talk about this later. Calm down."

"I think the coach is right, young lady."

Everyone turned to see Russell Garrison standing behind the bench. He had been watching the practice from the far end of the field.

"There's a lot of Pineview pride at stake in this tournament," he continued. "Why don't you girls listen to your coach? The team doesn't need any more trouble at this point."

"This is partly your fault, Mr. Garrison," Kelly retorted. "If it weren't for you, I wouldn't have missed the game yesterday. I was supposed to start, and I might have won a spot at the tournament."

"That was my mistake, and I apologize. But I'd curb my tongue if I were you, young lady."

"Why is it always me?" Kelly seemed on the verge of tears. "I'm tired of being everybody's scapegoat. I don't care about the dumb tournament."

"Then consider yourself off this team until further notice," Mr. Garrison said.

"Wait a minute, sir," said Kate. "I'm sure we can work this out."

"Maybe you'll listen to this kind of backtalk. But I won't. She's off, and that's final!"

11

Too Few Clues

There was a stunned silence on the field as Russell Garrison walked back toward the school. He turned and motioned for Kelly to follow.

"Let's go, young lady. I meant what I said."

Kelly edged closer to Coach Boggs.

"Go on," Kate whispered. "I'll talk to him later."

Kelly left the field slowly. No one spoke until she and the headmaster were out of sight.

"All right, girls. Run a few more laps and we'll call it a day," Kate said. "We have our first game of the tournament the day after tomorrow. Let's go."

The girls began jogging in silence. Kate walked over to George and Nancy.

"This is a coach's nightmare," she said. "You wait all your life to have a team this good. Now half the girls act as if they hate each other, and the headmaster yanks my backup goalie."

"He was overreacting," Nancy said. "The question is why?"

Kate shook her head. "I don't know. My problem isn't Russell Garrison. It's how to get this team ready for the day after tomorrow."

Kate went off to jog with the girls. It was as if she had to work off her frustration somehow. Jogging was the quickest way.

"What is it with Russell Garrison?" Nancy asked George. "It looked as though he was going out of his way to hurt the soccer team."

George shrugged, bewildered. "As far as I can see, winning the Canadian Cup would be great for the school."

Nancy shook her head. "Why do I have the funny feeling that there's more to this Canadian trip than just a soccer tournament?"

George sighed. "Beats me, Nancy." She stared across the field at the jogging girls. "Well, I'm the assistant coach of this team. I can't be the only one standing around."

George went off to join the others. Nancy decided to check out the gym.

When she reached the locker room, Kelly Lewis was just getting dressed. The once-confident girl looked very forlorn.

"Hi, Kelly," Nancy said quietly.

Kelly didn't answer. She pulled her blouse on and began brushing her hair.

"I don't know if you'll believe this," Nancy said, "but I'm sorry about what just happened."

"Why should you care? You're Janine's friend," Kelly retorted.

"I'm only trying to solve a jewel robbery," Nancy pointed out.

"Why not talk to Janine and her mother, then?"

"I have, and I don't think they were involved in the theft. If I'm wrong, I'll be the first to say so."

"That girl has been a thorn in my side for three years," Kelly said.

"That doesn't make her or her mother a jewel thief."

Kelly said nothing. She just took a deep breath and stared into the mirror.

"I really wanted to go to this tournament," she said. "You may not believe that, but I really wanted to play."

"I understand that," said Nancy. "Every player on a team is important."

"Yeah," Kelly said with an edge to her voice. "It's real important to keep the bench warm."

"Look at it this way. You're out there for practice every day. You've become a better player, and you've helped the other girls be better players. You're not the only fine athlete who's

100

sometimes had to sit out a game because there was someone a little better ahead of her."

Kelly looked at Nancy. "That's the hardest part. I love soccer. I always have. Not playing kills me"—she stopped in midsentence and looked away—"but I guess I've always known Janine is the better goaltender. And I'm jealous."

"That's normal," Nancy said. "The important thing is how you handle your jealousy."

"I guess I really haven't been helping the team," Kelly admitted. "And now I can't."

"Do you have any idea why Mr. Garrison would want you off the team?"

Kelly shrugged. "Because I lost my temper?"

"I don't think that's it."

"I told him yesterday in his office that I was going to miss the bus to Forsythe," Kelly said.

"You did? He told me he'd forgotten about the game."

"No, I kept telling him the bus was going to leave, but he wouldn't let me go. He threatened to suspend me from school if I walked out."

Nancy put her arm around the girl's shoulder. "It looks as if you've learned a hard lesson," she said.

Kelly looked at her. "You don't think Mr. Garrison will change his mind about kicking me off the team?"

"I don't think so," Nancy admitted. "But at least I can try to find out why he did it."

* * *

That night, Nancy and her father shared a bowl of popcorn in front of the fireplace after dinner. It was their first fire of the season. The flames warmed Nancy to her toes.

"What's missing is that one telling clue," she remarked to her father. "That one piece of hard evidence that I could use to build a case."

Carson Drew nodded. "I called Lieutenant Gerber at the police station today." He leaned forward to poke at the fire. "He said they've been watching carefully to see if the brooches turn up anywhere. So far they haven't."

"I doubt that the jewels have been moved yet," Nancy said. "The person who stole them is probably waiting for the right time to get rid of them."

"You may be right," her father said. "What about Garrison, the headmaster?"

Nancy swallowed some popcorn. "It's funny. The better I get to know him, the less I like him. But that doesn't make him a jewel thief."

"And the coach?" asked her father.

"Kate has the motive. She seems to have big personal problems, and she needs money. I'd hate to think she was involved in the theft, but I can't rule her out. I just can't imagine her pulling off that crime alone. In fact, whoever plotted this robbery had to hire a craftsman to make the fake brooches."

"Not an easy job," Mr. Drew said.

"No. In fact, I asked an expert about that. Even he couldn't tell me much about the art of lapidary."

"Who's that?"

"Jonathan Morse, the art teacher I told you about. Wonderful old man. Mr. Garrison is giving him a hard time, too."

"Is he a suspect?"

"Mr. Morse? Hardly. He thinks about only one thing—his teaching."

"Why is Garrison giving him a hard time?"

"Mr. Garrison thinks Mr. Morse is too old to teach," Nancy explained. "He wants him to retire."

Carson Drew thought that over for a moment. "Wouldn't that make a man like Morse ready to do anything?" he said. "Anything that would keep him teaching?"

Nancy just shook her head. How would the brooches help Jonathan Morse keep teaching? Besides, she couldn't imagine the kindly old man being involved in anything illegal.

"It's time I learned a little more about the art of lapidary," she said. "Maybe that will give me the clue I need."

Carson Drew nodded. "I know Ellen Sedgewick will be glad when this is over."

"Has her financial situation improved any?"

"It's getting there. If she can hang on a little longer, until she can sell some of her healthy stocks, she'll be all right."

"Or until an insurance payment comes through for the stolen jewels."

Carson Drew gave his daughter a surprised look.

"Sorry, Dad. I'm sure Mrs. Sedgewick is innocent, but I can't forget about that insurance money."

"Maybe you shouldn't go to Canada," he said. "You'll lose valuable time on your investigation."

"Dad, practically the entire cast of characters will be in Canada. With the crazy things that have been happening to the soccer team, I have this funny feeling that there still might be a link of some kind between the team and the robbery. I'm going."

The next morning Nancy arrived at the airport bright and early. She had stopped by the public library on the way and checked out several volumes on lapidary. Now she sat down with her tote bag full of books in the waiting room, prepared to read until the flight was called.

Several Pineview girls were already waiting with their parents. Finally, George appeared.

"You couldn't talk Bess into changing her mind and coming to Canada with us?" George asked Nancy.

"I didn't even try. I guess our friend just isn't much of a sports fan."

"Yeah," grumbled George, "just wait till she wants me to do something with her."

"Now, now," Nancy teased. "You wouldn't want her to go all the way to Canada just to be miserable, would you?"

"I guess not," George agreed. "What if it rained and she had to get wet?"

The two of them laughed. Meanwhile, more members of the soccer team had arrived. Janine appeared with her mother. The two of them took a seat at the back of the waiting room. Then Kate Boggs strode in, carrying an overnight case.

Nancy couldn't believe it. There was a spring in Kate's step and a glow on her face that Nancy hadn't seen before.

"Well, hello there," Nancy said. "You look like a coach with a mission."

"That's right," Kate said. "We're going to win the Canadian Cup. I won't let this team lose. Oh, George, Mr. Quinn is here with all the equipment. Could you make sure it gets onto the right flight? Wouldn't want our stuff to end up in Sweden."

George trotted off. Before she was even out of sight, Kate turned to Nancy and said, "I got some great news today. The coaching job I wanted came through. Starting next year I'll be coaching a Division Two college team—at almost twice the salary I'm getting here."

"Did you send George on that errand so that you could tell me this in private?"

"I don't want to make an official announcement until after the tournament. I've always wanted to coach at the college level. I'll also be able to get the other parts of my life straightened out."

"I'm very happy for you, Kate," Nancy said.

"Funny how things work out," said Kate. Her expression turned serious. "I didn't want to say anything before, but I've been having big problems with my mother. She's been very sick. I had to hire a nurse for her at home, and it cost a fortune. But last week I found a place that can take better care of her, and with my new job I'll be able to afford it. I've been hoping for this for months."

She smiled brightly. "All this was really distracting me from my work. But not now. Wouldn't the Canadian Cup be a great legacy to leave Pineview?"

Nancy nodded. She was happy that Kate's life was coming together, but Nancy didn't think this news would make her own job easier. Maybe she was making this trip for nothing.

12

All Aboard

George returned a few minutes later. She and Kate went off together to discuss some strategy for the game. Nancy decided to go over and greet Janine and her mother.

"Feeling any better today?" she asked Janine.

"A little," the girl said. She looked miserable.

"A lot of people are counting on you. You've got to leave the worrying to me and play soccer," Nancy told her.

"I told Mother she didn't have to come," Janine said.

"Nonsense," said Ellen Sedgewick. "I have nothing to hide. Let people think what they want. When this thing is over I'm sure everyone will know I'm innocent."

"Well said, Mrs. Sedgewick." Nancy turned back to Janine. "Remember," she told the young girl, "you let me worry about solving the case. You worry about winning a soccer tournament."

"I'll try," Janine promised.

Most of the team members had arrived by now. Many had their parents with them. A few faculty members were also waiting to board the plane. Electricity was in the air. Everyone could feel the excitement building.

Russell Garrison came into the waiting room alone and joined a group of teachers. He had on a wool topcoat, and his pointed features made him look like a character straight out of a spy movie. The cool nod he gave Nancy was definitely not friendly. She looked away from him and spotted Jonathan Morse hurrying in, lugging a huge suitcase behind him.

Nancy approached him immediately. "Hello, Mr. Morse. I'm surprised to see you here."

"I am, too," he said, wide-eyed. "But these girls are my students, you know. I want to see them win this tournament. Anyway, who knows? It may be my last hurrah."

"Oh, come on. You're supposed to teach my daughter someday."

"That's right. Well, at my age I shouldn't make promises anymore. But I'll try."

Nancy smiled as the teacher joined some other faculty members. She really liked Jonathan Morse. She made a mental note to talk to him some more in Canada, if she could. Nancy walked over to Kate and George.

"How's the summit meeting going?" she asked.

"Just about done for now," Kate said.

"Do you think the girls will be ready after everything that's happened?" Nancy asked.

"I'm counting on them to pull together when they realize where they are," Kate replied. "An awful lot depends on how Janine plays. If she's tested early and comes up with some big saves, it will give the whole team a lift."

"Did you talk to Mr. Garrison about Kelly?" Nancy asked.

"I tried to," Kate said. "But he told me not to bother. Right or wrong, he had to stick to his word, he said. Otherwise people would lose respect for him."

"Speaking of Mr. Garrison," George whispered, "here he comes."

The headmaster appeared before them. "I trust everyone is here and ready, Ms. Boggs," he said in his precise voice.

"Everyone except Kelly Lewis," Kate answered pointedly. Now that Kate had found another job, she didn't seem to care what the headmaster thought of her.

"Yes, that is unfortunate," Mr. Garrison said. "I'm sorry it had to happen."

"But not sorry enough to let her play."

Garrison closed his eyes for a moment. He seemed to be counting to ten silently, trying to control his temper. Then he said, "Is the equipment on the plane? Are we ready to go?"

"I checked everything myself," George said. "The equipment has already been loaded."

Garrison nodded. Then he turned toward Nancy. "Ms. Drew, I do hope you're on this trip purely as a soccer fan. I'd hate to think you're going all the way to Canada just to play detective."

"Would I do that, Mr. Garrison?" Nancy said with a smile.

"Yes, I believe you would." The headmaster flashed a tight smile of his own. Then he nodded and left, returning to the group of teachers.

"At least he lets you know where he stands," Kate remarked.

"I don't imagine he's an easy man to work for," Nancy said.

"He wouldn't win any popularity contests among the teachers and staff," said Kate. "I don't know how the trustees feel about him."

"If they didn't like him he'd be out of a job," said Nancy. "So he must be doing something right."

"The trick is to find it," George said.

Nancy drew in her breath and looked at George thoughtfully for a moment. "Be right back," she said. "I've got to make a phone call."

"It had better be quick," Kate said. "We're boarding in about two minutes."

Nancy headed for the nearest pay phone. She

110

made her call and returned to the waiting room just as the passengers began boarding the plane.

"Who'd you call?" George asked.

"Dad. I asked him to try to get me some information."

"You're too much, Nan," said George. "Why don't you relax for a couple of days and watch us win the Canadian Cup?"

"Don't you know me better than that by now?"

"I guess I should, huh?"

The two girls followed Kate onto the plane and took their seats, which were side by side. Everyone settled in quickly.

After takeoff, George turned in her seat to see down the aisle. She nudged Nancy. "Look at Kate," she said.

Nancy looked. Kate was walking up and down the aisle, giving each of the girls a pep talk and making them "think soccer" right from the beginning.

"I can't believe how she's changed," George said. "We need her like this if we're going to win. I hope she stays this way."

"She will," Nancy said, but she couldn't tell George why. She'd have to leave that up to Kate. She reached down and took some books from her tote bag.

"What are those?" George asked.

"Just some light reading I picked up this morning."

George looked over Nancy's shoulder. The

musty old volumes included color photographs of gemstones and jewelry crafting.

"Nan, don't you ever quit?" George asked.

"Nope. It's about time I learned more about the craft of jewelry making."

George sighed. "All right, give me one."

Nancy handed one of the books to George.

"What am I supposed to be looking for?" George asked.

"I'm not sure," Nancy said. "Something that will give us a clue about what the thief had to do to make the brooches. I know it's a long shot."

The two girls began reading the books in silence. At first George bravely turned page after page. But after fifteen minutes, her eyes began to close. She was snapped out of her doze when Nancy suddenly said, "I don't believe this. It was right under our noses the whole time."

"What was?" George looked over at her friend.

"A clue. Maybe *the* clue. The first real piece of evidence in this case."

"How can you find evidence in a dusty old book?"

Nancy turned to her friend. "The other day I was in Mr. Morse's art classroom, talking to him about the case," she explained. "When I left the room, I noticed some green greasy stuff on my right hand."

"So?" George asked.

"Look at this."

George looked at the book that Nancy was

holding open on her lap. A photograph on the page showed a green substance that looked exactly like what Nancy had described.

"That's the stuff," Nancy said. "Plastilene. According to this book, it's used in making everything from model cars to jewelry."

"Jewelry!"

"Uh-huh. You know what this means, George? Those fake brooches could have been made right at Pineview."

"You're right, Nan," George said. Then she gasped. "And if that's true, it would mean the thief would have to be Jonathan Morse!"

13

Hot Pursuit

Nancy looked at her friend. Then she looked down at the book again. There was no doubt that the green goop pictured on the page was what she had found on her hand.

"Plastilene is used for other kinds of model making, of course," she said hopefully to George. "It could just be a coincidence."

"Nancy!"

"I know. I just hate to think that Mr. Morse could be involved in this crime."

"Just 'involved'? Are you saying he worked with someone else?"

"Yes. He couldn't have pulled off this robbery alone. If he did make the fake jewels, he had to have an accomplice. In fact, I wouldn't be surprised if the accomplice was the one who started all this."

"But why would Jonathan Morse get involved? All he wants to do is teach at Pineview."

Nancy looked at her friend. "You may have answered your own question, George," she said.

Before George could reply, both girls were suddenly aware of someone standing over them in the aisle.

"Interesting reading matter, Ms. Drew," Mr. Garrison said. "I see you haven't followed my advice and given up. How foolish of me to think you were interested in soccer."

Nancy smiled at the headmaster. "I didn't know you were interested in lapidary, Mr. Garrison. Is it a hobby of yours?"

"Pineview is my only hobby, I'm afraid." His eyes bored into Nancy's. "I hope we don't have to have another talk, Ms. Drew," he said.

"I'm trying to solve a crime."

"And I've already told you to stop. My school has suffered enough from this scandal. Let's put it behind us, shall we?"

"I want that, too," Nancy said quietly. "We both want what's best for Pineview."

"I seriously doubt it," Mr. Garrison said. Then he turned to George. "And by the way, Ms. Fayne. Your job performance will be coming up for review soon. I hope you put Pineview before your personal friendships. Have a good day, ladies."

"I don't like that man at all," Nancy said after he had left.

"You wish he was the thief, not Jonathan Morse, don't you?" George remarked.

"George, you know me. I've never let personal feelings get in the way of a case before. I'm trying not to now. There's no evidence connecting Mr. Garrison to the theft. Only a couple of if's and maybe's. Certainly not enough to build a case on."

"What are you going to do about Jonathan Morse?"

Nancy craned her neck to look for the art teacher. She spotted him sitting by himself about six rows behind them. "I don't want to accuse him of anything," she said. "I think I'll just let him know I'm getting close to finding the thieves. Maybe then he'll talk to me."

She took her book and walked down the aisle to where the old man was sitting.

"Mind if I sit down for a minute, Mr. Morse?"

"You're always welcome, Ms. Drew," said the elderly man. "It's been a long time since I've flown. I'm thoroughly enjoying the flight."

"It's been a smooth one so far," said Nancy. She sat down and put the book in her lap. Its title was in plain sight of the art teacher.

"I have something here you might enjoy reading," she said.

"Really? What's that?"

"A book on lapidary, about crafting jewelry. I

remember your saying that you haven't had much experience with it."

The teacher squirmed a little in his seat.

"Well, no, I really haven't."

"I happened to pick this up at the library this morning. You can look at it if you like."

"I didn't know you were so interested in lapidary," said the teacher.

"I'm actually interested in solving a crime. I thought this might help. It gives me more information about jewelry making. For instance"— Nancy flipped open the book—"I learned that something called plastilene is often used in making fake jewelry. You know, when I left your room the other day I had some green stuff on my hand that looked a lot like plastilene."

Jonathan Morse coughed twice. He moved around again in his seat.

"Yes, we use plastilene for some of our projects," he said. "But I don't teach jewelry design."

"I know. I was just wondering what you did use it for."

"For model sculpting," the old man said.

"Is there a problem here, Jonathan?"

It was Russell Garrison again. He stood over Nancy in the aisle.

"No, sir. I was just discussing arts and crafts with our curious Ms. Drew."

"You mean the *nosy* Ms. Drew, don't you?"

"Now, Mr. Garrison, what's wrong with trying to pick up a little knowledge?" Nancy said. "You run a school. You should understand my curiosity."

"I've always heard that a *little* knowledge can be a dangerous thing," Mr. Garrison said. "Even you should know better than to badger a man like Mr. Morse."

"She wasn't badgering me, Russell," the old man said.

"Well, let's not argue," said Mr. Garrison. "Now, if you'll excuse us, Ms. Drew, I have some things to discuss with Jonathan."

Nancy had no choice but to leave. When she stood up, the headmaster immediately took her seat.

Shaking her head, Nancy returned to her seat next to George and told her friend what had happened.

"I'm still not sure who's a suspect and who isn't," Nancy said. "But something's got to happen soon."

"Come on, Nan," said George. "We're going to Canada to try to win a soccer championship. I hope the girls' concern over this case doesn't spoil their game."

"I hope it doesn't, either. But I can't help feeling that the soccer team is somehow connected to the whole thing."

"Oh, no," George groaned. "Not again."

"But that's the problem with this case," Nancy continued. "Too many feelings, and not enough facts."

For the rest of the flight Nancy and George relaxed. The landing was a smooth one. The team was to take a bus from the airport to the Clayton-Bagdall School, several miles north of Canada's Niagara Falls. The school had a large stadium and would host the four-team, single-elimination tournament.

When they arrived inside the air terminal, Coach Boggs gave George the big duffel bag that contained all the special equipment. George tossed the strap over her shoulder without complaining, even though the bag was very heavy.

"Try to imagine Bess lugging this thing," she said to Nancy.

"Not in a million years." Nancy laughed.

The team would be staying in a dormitory at the school, while the parents, faculty, and friends would be housed in a hotel half a mile away.

Nevertheless, everyone went to the school first so the team could get settled. The semifinal game was set for the following afternoon. Kate called a light practice on one of the school's playing fields for late in the day, just to loosen the girls up.

"George, go ahead and separate the brand-new game uniforms and equipment from the practice gear," Kate said. "You can use my room."

"I'll help you," Nancy offered.

While they were busy working, Russell Garrison walked in.

"I trust the rooms are satisfactory," he said to the coach.

119

"Mm-hmm. We're all set," Kate answered.

"I guess I should wish you luck, Ms. Boggs. I'm sure you'll do your best for Pineview."

Then the headmaster spotted Nancy.

"She isn't supposed to be here," he said. "These dorm rooms are just for the team."

"She's just helping us with the equipment," Kate explained. "She has a room at the hotel, same as you."

Garrison frowned. "Yes, fine. Well, good luck."

"That guy doesn't miss a trick," George muttered as he left.

"He's pretty thorough," Kate said. "I'll say that much for him."

Nancy stayed with the team through practice. "They weren't bad at all," she said to George as the girls went off to shower. "In fact, they ran so hard they made *me* hungry. You want to go with me to the hotel for some supper?"

"The team's eating here in the school dining hall," George said. "I need to make sure they get enough food in their stomachs. But I can meet you later, if you want."

"Great! We'll have our own celebration *before* the games." Nancy patted her friend on the back and left for the hotel.

As she entered the hotel lobby, Nancy thought she saw someone duck quickly into a rear elevator alcove. The person's furtive movements made Nancy suspicious. She ran toward the alcove just in time to see the door close on an elevator.

But that didn't stop Nancy. "The stairs," she murmured. She ran through a heavy door and up several flights of concrete steps, checking each floor to see whether the elevator had stopped. As she puffed up to the fifth floor, she heard the elevator door open and someone hurry out. She threw open the stairway door and ran into the hallway. She caught a quick glimpse of a girl before she entered a room and slammed the door.

Nancy stopped dead in her tracks. Was the fleeing girl really Kelly Lewis?

14

Carried Away

Nancy paused to catch her breath. What would Kelly be doing there? Nancy didn't think Mr. Garrison could forbid her to come to Canada on her own, but he could probably make things pretty rough for her if he chose.

Nancy had to find out. She went up to the door and knocked.

There was no answer. She knocked again. Still there was no sound from inside the room. Nancy decided to take a chance.

"Open up, Kelly," she shouted. "It's Nancy Drew. Come on, Kelly. I saw you."

She listened. Someone was walking slowly toward the door. She heard the lock snap, and then the door opened. Kelly Lewis stood there. She was almost trembling.

"Why did you run?" Nancy asked as she went inside.

"I didn't want anyone to know I was here," the girl said. "I told everyone at school that I was going home for a few days. I never told my parents I was kicked off the team, though. I was too ashamed. And I had to see the team play for the Canadian Cup."

"That's the only reason you're here?"

"What other reason is there? I've been part of this team for three years. I can't just forget about them when they're playing for the championship."

"Mr. Garrison can't stop you from coming here on your own time," Nancy said.

"No, but I'm cutting classes, and I lied to my parents. He can make it tough for me. Maybe even get me expelled."

"And is this worth the risk?"

"To see the team win and be a part of it in a small way? Yes, it's worth it."

Nancy smiled sadly at the girl who had made things so rough for Janine Sedgewick.

"Well, if it's any comfort, your secret is safe with me," Nancy said. "Why don't you call your parents and tell them what happened? They'll back you up if Mr. Garrison tries to cause you more trouble."

Kelly sat on the edge of the bed. "Let me think about it," she said. "I know I'm going to watch the games. No one is going to stop me from doing that."

"Then I'll see you there," Nancy said. "Tell you what. If I have some time tonight, I'll come over for a while and keep you company."

"Thanks, Nancy. I'd appreciate that."

Nancy went back to her own room and called her father.

"I found out what you wanted to know," he said.

"Does this mean anything?" he asked after he'd given Nancy the information.

"I'm not sure," she replied. "It may help, if some of my other theories turn out to be right. But there are still some missing pieces. Mainly, the whereabouts of the jewels."

She said goodbye to her father and lay down on her bed to read more about jewelry making until George joined her.

"The girls are finally pulling together," George announced as she entered the room at seven o'clock. "You should have seen them at supper. Kate's enthusiasm seems to be rubbing off. I don't know if she realizes it or not, but when she was down, the whole team was down."

"I think she knew," Nancy said. "It was just that she couldn't do anything about it for a while."

George looked her friend in the eye. "Nan, do you know something I don't know?"

"Maybe. But nothing I can tell you now."

"Oh, boy! Another mystery," said George.

"This one won't last long," Nancy promised, "but I really can't talk about it."

George knew better than to try to persuade Nancy to tell her a secret. "Okay, okay," she said. "So let's order some food up here and just watch television for a while. I don't want to have to think about anything for the rest of the night."

At nine-thirty, after a big meal and a nice chat, George stretched and said, "Time to go home. It wouldn't look good for the assistant coach to break curfew."

Nancy smiled. "Good luck tomorrow," she said. "I'll be rooting for you."

After George left, Nancy decided to order a cup of hot chocolate for dessert and then get a good night's sleep.

After she placed her order she remembered Kelly. Oh, well, she decided, when the hot chocolate comes I'll take it to Kelly's room.

Ten minutes later there was a knock on the door. Nancy opened the door. It was the hot chocolate, all right. But holding the tray was none other than Russell Garrison.

"Ms. Drew, I'm here with a peace offering." He flashed her a surprisingly warm smile. "It's time to end this hostility between us."

For once, Nancy was speechless.

"How did you know I'd ordered hot chocolate?"

"Always questions." Mr. Garrison smiled. "I

know, I know. That's why you're a detective. I just happened to be in the hallway when the waiter from room service arrived. I asked him what I had to do to get a cup of coffee. He told me he'd get it for me right after he delivered the hot chocolate to you. I offered to do that for him. And here I am."

Nancy couldn't believe how hard Mr. Garrison was trying to be charming. "Well, then, I guess I have no choice but to invite you in," Nancy said with a little laugh.

Russell Garrison stepped inside. "Of course, if you prefer, we could go down to the lobby. But I would like to talk."

"That's okay," Nancy said. "Please sit down."

The headmaster sat at a small table in the corner of the room. Nancy sat opposite him.

"Ms. Drew, I did some checking on you. You have quite a reputation in River Heights."

"I guess I should be flattered that you checked up on me."

"Well, I'm sure you've been checking up on me," Mr. Garrison replied.

"So I have." Nancy smiled.

Garrison laughed easily. "I know I've been rude lately," he said, "but you must understand that this jewel theft has upset me greatly. With so much finger pointing, it's almost as though everyone is a suspect."

"You've done some finger pointing yourself, Mr. Garrison. You haven't exactly made Mrs.

Sedgewick or her daughter feel very good. Not to mention Coach Boggs."

"I know." He sighed. "None of us is perfect. Maybe I was hoping this thing would be solved quickly. Ellen Sedgewick seemed the most likely suspect, especially when I learned about her money problems. Unfortunately, I'm not a detective."

Nancy checked her watch. It was nearly ten o'clock. She remembered her promise to visit Kelly, but she certainly couldn't tell Mr. Garrison that Kelly was in the hotel.

"You know, Ms. Drew," Mr. Garrison continued, keeping his eyes closely trained on her. "No matter what you think of me, Pineview is a very highly rated school. That's something I'm very proud of and always have been."

Nancy yawned, covering her mouth with her hand. What was Mr. Garrison up to? He seemed to be going on and on. As Nancy sipped her hot chocolate, the room seemed to grow warmer. Almost too warm. She felt like going to sleep right then and there, but she had promised to visit Kelly.

"Mr. Garrison, what is . . . uh . . . the point of all this?" she mumbled. She suddenly felt so tired she could hardly get the words out.

"I just wanted to clear the air," he said. "To show you there are no hard feelings on my part. I know I haven't been very helpful with your investigation. For that I apologize. When we get

127

back to Pineview I'll try to help in any way I can to get to the bottom of all this. I really want to see this case solved."

While Garrison droned on and on about his good intentions, Nancy sipped her chocolate and grew even sleepier. Now she could hardly keep her eyes open. The room began to spin. Mr. Garrison was just a blur across the table from her. She started to pick up the hot chocolate again, but the cup fell from her hand.

"Getting sleepy, Ms. Drew?" she heard Mr. Garrison say. "You must be tired from all your hard detective work. A good night's sleep is probably what you need, but this hotel can be noisy. I know a better place. A place where no one will disturb you and you can sleep as long as you wish."

Nancy sensed Mr. Garrison getting up. She felt him put her coat over her shoulders and practically lift her to her feet. She could barely walk as he helped her out of the room. In the split second before she lost consciousness, she realized what had happened.

Russell Garrison had drugged her.

15

A Close Call

When Nancy next opened her eyes it was daylight. She was groggy and a bit dizzy. In her confusion she turned over to go back to sleep. But just before she dozed off, she remembered what had happened.

She sat up suddenly. Her head started spinning, and she had to lie down again. Then, slowly, she propped herself up in bed. It was only then that she realized she wasn't in her hotel room.

The place she was in looked like a cabin. It had only one room, and it was cold. She had three or four blankets piled on top of her, and she was still wearing her coat.

Slowly her head started to clear. She looked at

her watch. It was nearly twelve o'clock! She had been sleeping for more than twelve hours.

Standing up finally, she steadied herself by leaning on a small table near the bed.

Where was she?

When her head cleared enough for her to walk, she opened the door and looked outside. All she could see in every direction was forest. Several inches of snow had fallen during the night. It was a beautiful sight, but it was also frightening.

She had to get out of there, but she had no idea how far she would have to walk to find help.

Nancy took the warmest blanket and threw it over her coat. Then she stepped outside into the cold.

The crisp, fresh air cleared her head even more. It was important to find her way back to town as quickly as she could. The soccer game was due to start at two o'clock.

Mr. Garrison hadn't had time to take her very far from the hotel, she reasoned. He would have worried about being missed.

After looking around, Nancy decided to head south, using the sun as a beacon.

She wasn't very far from the cabin when she noticed some tracks in the snow—a snowmobile. That must have been how Mr. Garrison brought her there. She began following the tracks.

Gradually, the woods thinned out. Nancy found herself on a wider trail meant for cross-country skiers and snowmobilers. She followed the trail for nearly an hour before she finally reached a two-lane highway.

Nancy couldn't wait for a car to pass by. The deserted road seemed to run north and south. She began walking south.

It was ten minutes before she heard a car coming from behind her. Though she knew the dangers of hitchhiking, Nancy had no choice but to flag the car down. There were two young women inside, and two pairs of skis were tied to the car's roof.

"How far are we from the Clayton-Bagdall School?" Nancy asked.

"Isn't that the one near the Falls?" one of the girls said.

"Yes, that's it," said Nancy.

"It's about an hour away."

"Oh, boy," Nancy said. "You wouldn't be headed that way, would you?"

"In that general direction," said the driver. She was a blond girl who looked like the skiers Nancy had seen on television.

"I've got to get back there," Nancy said. "Could you possibly give me a ride?"

The driver looked at the other girl, who was a little chubby and didn't look like a skier.

"Hop in," the other one said.

"I'm Anne," the driver introduced herself as they drove. "This is my friend, Joan. We're heading for the mountains for our first ski trip of the season. And what brings you here, may we ask?"

When Nancy told them some of what had happened to her, the two girls could hardly believe her. Still, they were friendly enough. By the time they reached the end of the highway, they had agreed to take Nancy the extra eight miles to the school.

"You really should go to the police with your story," Anne said.

"The police will know about this soon enough," Nancy said. "I hope by then I'll have more to show them than just a little kidnapping."

"A little kidnapping?" cried Joan. "If that happened to me, I'd be petrified."

"You're right," Nancy agreed. "It wasn't very pleasant."

"Some of those hunters' and trappers' cabins are in the middle of nowhere," Anne said. "That guy could have dropped you off in a place you could never have gotten out of."

"Alive," added Joan.

"Please." Nancy shuddered at the thought. "I realized that when I first looked outside. But I didn't think he'd taken me very far."

"You were still lucky," said Anne. "You could have walked in the wrong direction. If you had gone north or east, you'd still be walking."

"And there are wolves out there," Joan said.

"Hey," Nancy protested. "You girls sure are full of good cheer."

"We try," said Anne. "We're almost there, Nancy. Where do you want us to drop you?"

Nancy checked her watch. "Do you mind taking me to the soccer stadium? The game's already in progress. I want to see if act two of this drama is going to be played out there."

"We've come this far," Anne said cheerfully.

A large crowd had gathered for the semifinal games. The host team, Clayton-Bagdall, had won the opener. Now Pineview was playing the Secord School in the second game. By the time Nancy and her two rescuers arrived it was well past three o'clock.

"I can't thank you two enough." Nancy jumped out of the car. "But I've got to get over there fast and find out what's happening."

"As long as we're here, maybe we'll watch for a few minutes," said Anne. "I used to play this game a long time ago."

"You sound like an old lady," said Joan.

"I feel old after listening to Nancy tell us about *her* day!" Anne replied.

The large crowd was shouting with excitement as Nancy made her way between the packed bleachers to the sidelines. She could see Kate pacing up and down nearby. The coach was shouting encouragement, giving orders, almost directing traffic on the field.

133

George was on one knee in front of the bench, acting more like a cheerleader than an assistant coach. Nancy walked right up and knelt down beside George.

"How are we doing?" she asked, as if nothing had happened.

"Tied at two to two, about four minutes left," George said without looking. Then she did a double take. "Nan, where in the world have you been? I looked all over for you, right up until game time."

"It's a long story, and not a pretty one. Have you seen Russell Garrison?"

"Not since early this morning, when I was looking for you. What's this about the two of you having hot chocolate last night?"

"What else did he tell you?"

"Nothing. Just that he ran into you in the lobby. He said he brought you hot chocolate as a peace offering. Then he said you got tired and went to sleep."

"I was tired, all right. Thanks to some knockout drops supplied by Russell Garrison. He even took me for a midnight ride."

"What?" said George. She looked at Nancy in disbelief.

Nancy nodded. "Garrison wanted me out of the way for some reason. Now, think, George. Has anything out of the ordinary happened today involving the soccer team?"

George thought for a moment. "Well, we had

134

some vandalism. Kate figures it was a Secord prank."

"What kind of vandalism?" There was an urgent tone to Nancy's voice.

"Someone got into the equipment bag and messed up our uniforms a little."

"What do you mean, 'messed up'?"

"Spray-painted some of the shirts, punctured a couple of practice balls, and slashed the knee pads Janine was going to wear."

Nancy thought for a minute. "How did they slash the knee pads?"

"They slit them down the middle and then pulled them apart. Janine's wearing some old practice pads, but she's playing a great game."

Just then there was a roar from the crowd. Two Secord forwards were breaking in on goal. One of them booted the ball toward the left corner of the net. Janine took two quick steps and dived! She made an excellent one-hand save. Then she smothered the ball, got up, and kicked it down the length of the field.

With time running out, Pineview got the ball at midfield. Karen Phelps passed to Paula LeGere, who dribbled down the left side toward the Secord goal.

"Center it! Now!" Kate shouted.

Paula pivoted and booted the ball with her left foot. It drifted toward the net. The Secord goaltender came out to try to catch it. But Janie Fryer got there a split second before her and headed the ball past the startled goalie. The ball sailed into the net. Pineview had scored to take a 3–2 lead with just a minute left.

The crowd stood and cheered for the entire final minute as Pineview turned back a last-ditch Secord drive. Janine made another nice save and kicked the ball high and deep just before the whistle sounded. Pineview had won! They were in the finals!

All the girls gathered around Janine at the goal. Kate and George joined them in celebrating, but Nancy knew there was little time to waste. She ran onto the field and grabbed George by the shoulders.

"Come on. We've got work to do."

"Nan, give me a few minutes to enjoy this. We're in the finals!"

"I know. I know," Nancy said. "But you'll have to celebrate later."

"Why?"

"You know those slashed knee pads you were telling me about?"

"What about them?"

"I'll bet you anything that Mrs. Sedgewick's brooches were hidden inside those pads!"

16

Cut to the Chase

George didn't have time to react to what Nancy had told her. Nancy had already grabbed her hand and was pulling her off the field, through the excited crowd. They raced out to the parking lot.

"I hope we're not too late," Nancy said.

"For what?" asked George, who was still stunned.

Nancy headed toward a line of cars waiting to leave the parking lot for the highway.

"There they are," Nancy shouted. "Hey, Anne! Joan!"

The two young women had the car windows rolled up and didn't hear Nancy. There was just one car ahead of them in line. Then they'd be gone. Nancy kept running while she shouted.

The car in front of the skiers moved out of the parking lot. Anne and Joan were next. It didn't look as if Nancy would make it. But just as the car started off, Nancy came up from behind and slapped the car's rear fender with her open hand. The car stopped short. Joan stuck her head out of the passenger's window.

"Nancy! What is going on?"

"We need a fast ride to the Pirot Hotel. It's right down the road. Could you please give us a lift?"

"Hop in," Anne said from behind the wheel.

Nancy and George climbed into the backseat as Anne swung the car out onto the highway.

"Here we go," Nancy said. "By the way, this is George. George, Anne and Joan."

"Strange way to meet," said Joan. "Where are we going, to a fire?"

"No," Nancy said. "We're going to catch a jewel thief."

Nancy could see Anne stare at her in the rearview mirror. "You're kidding," she said.

"I hope not. I also hope we're not too late."

Anne stepped on the gas. In a matter of minutes she was pulling into the hotel parking lot.

"Could you wait here a minute in case we need help?" Nancy jumped out, shouting, "Thanks!" She raced into the lobby.

The first person she saw was Jonathan Morse, who was just walking out of the hotel. He looked surprised to see Nancy in such a hurry.

"My dear," he said. "Did our team win?"

"Where's Mr. Garrison?" she asked. The old man jumped.

"Ms. Drew! What's the problem?"

Nancy knew it was time to shoot straight, though in a way she hated to do it.

"Mr. Morse, I know you made the fake jewels. I also know Mr. Garrison has the real ones. They were smuggled over the border in the goalie's knee pads. You can make this easier if you tell me where Garrison has gone. Otherwise, the police will find out. Either way, it's over."

The old man put a trembling hand up to his face. "I didn't want to do it. He made me. He said I'd lose my job if I didn't—"

"I know that," Nancy interrupted. "But, please, where is he now?"

"He left five minutes ago. He's meeting a buyer at Niagara Falls."

"Thanks. And don't worry. We know the pressure he put on you."

What a perfect place to fence stolen jewels, right in the middle of a crowd of tourists, Nancy said to herself as she raced back to the car.

Anne and Joan were waiting for her in the hotel driveway. Nancy peered into the window. "I hate to ask you this, but . . ."

"Hop in," Anne said with a shrug.

"Would you rather have Nancy drive?" George said. "She's an old pro at this."

"Are you game?" Anne asked her friend.

"Why not?" Joan replied. "It can't be any more dangerous than skiing."

Joan jumped into the backseat with George. Anne slid into the passenger seat, and Nancy got behind the wheel.

"Where are we headed?" Anne asked.

"Niagara Falls, unless we can catch him before he gets there."

"Somehow this doesn't sound like a pleasure trip," Joan remarked.

Nancy started weaving through the traffic. She was an expert driver, not a reckless one. She didn't want to be stopped by the police now.

Once outside of town she was able to speed up. As she drove, she filled in the still-bewildered women on what was happening.

"I still can't believe Jonathan Morse is involved in this," George said.

"He was being blackmailed, with the only thing that means anything to him in the world," Nancy said. "Teaching at Pineview. I think the police will go easy with him."

"But not with Garrison," George remarked.

"We've got to be careful with that guy," Nancy said. "If he had pulled this off without a hitch, I'm sure he'd have returned to Pineview a much richer man, someone who probably wouldn't have tried something like this again. Now he knows he can't return. That could make him very dangerous."

As Nancy neared the Falls, the traffic picked up

140

again. The flow of tourists to the Falls was almost as heavy as the flow of the water. They headed for the main parking lot near Horseshoe Falls on the Canadian side. While Nancy fought through the traffic, George suddenly yelled, "There he is! In that red sedan up ahead!"

Nancy craned her neck and spotted Garrison in the red car. The car was about a hundred feet ahead of them, already entering the parking lot.

"Try to keep an eye on him when he gets out of the car," she told the others. "At least see where he parks."

"This is for real, isn't it?" Anne said.

"Do you think he's carrying a gun?" asked Joan.

That was something Nancy hadn't even considered.

"I doubt it," she said. "I don't think he operates that way. And I don't think he expected to be caught."

"He's parking," George said. "There's the car, in the right-hand corner of the lot."

"Good girl," said Nancy. Then she turned to Anne and Joan. "When we park, George and I will go after him. I don't want to put either of you in any more danger. But if we don't nab him and he comes back to his car, will you alert a police officer or security guard? There seem to be enough of them around."

As Nancy maneuvered the car into the lot, she saw Garrison walking quickly toward one of the paths that led to the viewing area beside the Falls.

"George, let's go now. Anne, you can pull the car over near his."

Before Anne could answer, George and Nancy were out of the car and running after Russell Garrison. When they reached the top of the steps they saw the headmaster below. He was talking to another man, just in front of the admission gate to the viewing area.

Garrison was carrying a small shoulder bag. "Look. The jewels must be in there," Nancy said to George. They saw the other man reach into the breast pocket of his jacket and pull a white envelope partway out. Then he slid it in again.

"That must be the money," Nancy said. "We've got to stop Garrison before he gives that guy the bag."

The two men began moving back, away from the crowd of tourists. Nancy started after them.

"Mr. Garrison!" Nancy shouted.

The headmaster looked around. He seemed unsure whether someone was shouting at him.

"Here! Mr. Garrison!"

Then he spotted her. His face flashed a mixture of surprise, hatred, and panic, all at the same time. He tucked the bag under his arm and started walking quickly toward the path that led under the Falls. The second man, realizing something was wrong, quickly disappeared into the crowd.

Nancy and George pushed their way through the crowd toward the gate. There was a line to get in. But Garrison barged through it to the gate. He jumped over the turnstile, right in front of a startled ticket taker.

Nancy and George didn't have time for formalities, either. They leapt over the turnstile after the headmaster. "I hope that ticket taker calls security right away," George muttered.

Garrison started to run. He carried the bag of jewels under his arm like a football player and used his free hand to push people out of his way. Nancy and George raced after him as he headed down the narrowing path toward the Falls. The sound of the cascading water grew louder. The mist created by the constant spray rose around them like a rain cloud.

As they chased the fleeing headmaster, George gasped, "What if he throws the jewels into the Falls?"

Nancy's eyes widened. If the headmaster did that, the jewels would be lost forever. "Let's hope he's too greedy," she panted. "Come on, George. Step on it!"

The path suddenly narrowed and the large number of tourists slowed Garrison down. A group of visitors taking pictures blocked his path. He tried to fight his way through them, but then he realized he couldn't make it. Out of breath, he turned to find himself face-to-face with Nancy and George.

"So this is how it ends, eh?" he said, smiling. The roar from the Falls had become almost deafening by now. "I must say, you are a stubborn young lady. Maybe I should have made your hot chocolate even stronger."

"That's not your style, Mr. Garrison." Nancy tried to keep her voice calm. "I'm sure it wasn't easy doing what you did."

Garrison laughed. "Don't be so sure. My one shot at the brass ring? If I was willing to sacrifice a teacher like Jonathan Morse, what makes you think I would have spared you?"

"Let's not argue over details, Mr. Garrison," Nancy said. "The point is, it's finished. If you'll come quietly and turn yourself in to the police, maybe they'll go easier on you."

"Sure, and simply let me return to Pineview and live happily ever after."

"You and I both know that's impossible," Nancy said.

"You and I both know something else, too," answered Mr. Garrison with a smile.

"What's that?"

"All I have to do is toss this bag over that railing and you don't have a shred of evidence. It'll be my word against yours."

"What about Jonathan Morse?"

"Do you really think he'll admit his guilt with his job at stake?" Garrison began to edge closer to the rail.

Nancy moved quickly to cut him off. But Garrison spun to his left and threw the bag toward the rail.

Nancy lunged, but the bag was beyond her reach. She watched her entire case heading into the Falls. And she could do nothing to stop it.

17

The Canadian Cup

As Nancy turned, she saw George take a big step and leap high into the air. It seemed impossible for her to reach the bag. But instead of trying to grab it with her hands, George did a perfect soccer scissors kick. She caught the bag with her foot and flipped it over her head as she fell backward.

Russell Garrison, startled, just stood there as Nancy pounced on the bag and clutched it under her arm. Then, as he began moving toward her, a security guard and a police officer rushed up and grabbed him.

"What's going on here?" the security guard demanded.

"They tried to steal my bag," Mr. Garrison said quickly.

"His bag," said Nancy, "contains two stolen brooches from the Pineview School. Their soccer team is playing for the Canadian Cup at the Clayton-Bagdall School. People there can back up what I'm saying."

"The jewels are mine, I tell you," Mr. Garrison growled.

"If they're yours, buddy, how come you were running away from two young girls?"

This time Mr. Garrison didn't answer. "Let's go," said the police officer. "We'll clear this up at the school. If the brooches are yours, you have nothing to worry about, right?"

The police officer and Garrison followed Nancy, George, and the security guard. As they walked toward the parking lot, Nancy nudged George in the ribs.

"That was a better save than I ever saw Janine make."

George smiled. "I taught her everything she knows."

After dinner, several members of the Pineview crowd gathered in the lobby of the hotel. Kate was there. So were Ellen and Janine Sedgewick, as well as a couple of the other girls from the team. There was a big game to play the next day, but by now everyone had heard that Russell Garrison and Jonathan Morse had been arrested.

"Mr. Morse was a victim," Nancy said. "He saw his life being ripped away from him by a

147

ruthless man. He felt he had no choice but to make the fake brooches for his boss."

"What made you suspect Garrison?" Ellen Sedgewick asked. "Was it because he seemed so eager to pin the theft on me?"

"Not really," Nancy answered. "At first I thought he just wanted a fast solution so the school would stop getting bad publicity."

Nancy looked around at her audience and smiled. "He also had what I thought was a perfect alibi. Why would a thief ask for an expert to examine the fakes in front of everyone? After all, if the switch hadn't been discovered at the auction, the phony jewels would have been bought, and Mr. Garrison could have sold the real ones. The switch might not have been discovered for years, if ever."

"So why did he invite Mr. Ray to the ball?" Janine asked.

"Mr. Ray told me that no one realized he planned to inspect the jewels again. Mr. Garrison simply asked Mr. Ray to write down the amount the jewels were worth and seal the appraisal in the envelope. He had no idea how thorough Mr. Ray would be."

"Why did Mr. Garrison steal the brooches?" Kate asked.

"That's what I wondered," Nancy said. "So I had my father check on Garrison's personal finances. According to his bank statements, he was barely making it from paycheck to paycheck. I guess after all those years of socializing with wealthy parents and alumnae, the glitz and glamour of money became too tempting."

"I still don't understand how he managed to make the switch," Mrs. Sedgewick said.

"When you first brought the jewels to the school to set up the auction, Mr. Garrison had a stack of publicity photos taken. He had a number of copies of the photos made. That gave Jonathan Morse just what he needed to make the fakes. The switch, of course, was made on the day of the auction. Mr. Garrison made sure he was never alone with the jewels. He let the one man no one would suspect make the switch for him."

"I remember now," Mrs. Sedgewick said. "We were getting ready to put the jewels back into the safe, and Jonathan Morse began admiring them. He asked if he could look at them in a better light. He went over to the window in the corner."

"Right," said Nancy. "And because no one would ever think of Jonathan Morse as a possible thief, he made the switch right under your noses."

"That's incredible," Janine said.

"It's when you don't think a crime will happen that it can happen most easily," Nancy said.

"Then who pushed you into the boiler room?" George asked.

"That was Garrison. He must have followed me

from his office. Strong-arm tactics aren't really his style, but maybe he thought a push would scare me off the case."

"Fat chance," said George.

"There's one thing I don't understand. Why did he come to Canada with the soccer team?" Kate asked. "Why not just sell the jewels somewhere around River Heights?"

"There was too much police activity around River Heights," Nancy said. "If the theft hadn't been discovered, Garrison might have sold them there. But with everyone looking for suspects, he didn't want to take a chance."

She turned to George. "Remember the day Janine's knee pads were missing? Dear old Mr. Morse was sewing the brooches into them. Garrison knew you were saving those new pads for the tournament in Canada."

"One more thing," said George. "Why did Russell Garrison try so hard to break the team's morale?"

"Because he felt a divided team would more easily explain the vandalizing of the equipment. Besides, if the team lost the first game in the tournament, everyone would return to Pineview sooner, including Garrison. Except that he would have been a lot richer than when he left River Heights."

"I'm glad it's over," Ellen Sedgewick said. "Fortunately, I am now in a position to offer the jewels for auction again. All the money will go to Pineview, with a portion, of course, reserved for the soccer program."

"Speaking of soccer," Kate said, "we have another important game to play tomorrow. I suggest that everyone get a good night's sleep. We can all rest easier now, anyway, thanks to Nancy."

"Just a minute," Nancy said. "There's one more thing I think you all should know. Wait here. I'll be right back."

The others looked at one another. They wondered what Nancy was up to. Five minutes later, the detective returned with Kelly Lewis at her side.

"Here's a member of the team who was so loyal she risked getting expelled from Pineview to come here and watch the games."

Kelly blushed, but the girls from the team rushed up to her. Kate joined them.

"Now that we know about Russell Garrison," the coach said, "I don't see any reason for you to stay off the team. I'd be proud to have you suit up for the game tomorrow."

Kelly looked around. She didn't know what to say. Janine came up to her and extended her hand.

"And I need you there behind me," she said. "I never told you this before, but having you competing with me these last three years has

151

made me a better player. Even in the games, I always knew I could go all out because if anything happened, you'd be there to take my place."

The two girls hugged each other.

Kate threw a fist into the air. "And tomorrow at this time we'll have won the Canadian Cup!"

It was an almost magical game for Pineview. The girls were relaxed and confident. Their passes danced from foot to foot as though there were magnets on their shoes. They outplayed Clayton-Bagdall from the opening whistle.

Kate had told the girls before the game that she would be leaving Pineview. She had explained that, though she didn't like to leave the team, she felt she had to pursue her own goals. Today the girls were playing for Kate.

By halftime, it was a 3–0 game. Pineview was completely in command. Nancy stood behind the bench and cheered as the score went to 5–1, with just five minutes left. Then Coach Boggs pulled Janine and put Kelly in her place at the net.

With Janine and the others cheering her on, Kelly made one outstanding save after another in the closing minutes. Pineview won the game by a score of 6–1. They had done it!

When the game ended, the large crowd cheered wildly as the Pineview girls took a victory lap around the field. They were led by Janine and Kelly, who held the large silver cup aloft. Then the girls hoisted Kate onto their shoulders and gave her a victory ride. It was a wonderful moment in Pineview history.

There was a big dinner planned that night at a local restaurant. The next morning the team would visit Niagara Falls, and they would fly home that afternoon.

Everyone thanked Nancy again for all she had done, but she surprised them when she said she would have to miss the victory dinner.

"I'll join you in the morning to see the Falls. Our last visit was a little less than satisfying. Now I want to go there and play tourist."

"What about tonight?" asked George. "I can't believe you're going to miss the dinner."

"There's a very sad old man who needs to be bailed out of jail," she said. "I called Dad. He's taking care of the details. We've made arrangements to get Mr. Morse on an evening flight home. He's been through enough."

"Well, then, you can come to the dinner."

"Maybe I'll get there for dessert. But there are also a couple of weekend skiers who trusted me enough to give me a ride and then let me take them on a not-so-merry chase."

"Anne and Joan! I'd forgotten about them," George said.

"I promised I'd call to let them know how everything turned out. Without them, Garrison might have succeeded. I think I owe them a dinner."

"They accepted?"

"Yes, but they made me promise something first."

"What's that?" asked George.

"They made me promise to forget I was a detective," Nancy said, laughing.